Captain Tomahawk and the Sky-Lion

anthempoet.com

First Edition: September 2014

Original Illustration by Olin Kidd
olinthekidd.com

Published by the Author.
Lisle, Illinois, 60532

Cataloging-in-Publication Data

Dalton, Marty S.

Captain tomahawk and the sky-lion / Marty S. Dalton.
−1st ed.

ISBN-13 978-1-49-934202-4 (paperback)
ISBN-10 1499342020
BISAC: FIC028060 / FIC042010 / FIC002000

Printed in the United States of America

Captain Tomahawk and the Sky-Lion

By

Marty S. Dalton

FOR MY FRIENDS

THE MIDDLE

CHapTeR 1

Sometimes, the most unlikely of heroes have the most wonderful of adventures, and when they do, they always start in the middle.

"Oh, no, no, no! Not now! Not now!" Captain Anna cried as the Sky-Lion careened towards the ground below, sparking heavily.

She looked over her right shoulder to see that one of the wings had been shot clean through and was scraping against the side of the vessel. The metal on metal was sending a flurry of sparks into the air, dangerously close to the main sails. "Not now!" she kept repeating.

Now, indeed, would be a terrible time to crash-land. For at the moment, she was crossing new territory. She was flying low over the Highsand Desert, the most deadly and dangerous—not to mention hot and humungous—desert in the world.

She was only a few hundred feet in the air when the missile had hit the Sky-Lion's starboard-side wing. This would be a truly disastrous place to crash, leagues and leagues from anything or anyone who could rescue her.

She pulled up as hard as she could on the controls. If she could just manage to make it back over the water, she could float the Sky-Lion home. But it did no good; the airship kept losing altitude. In front of her was a giant dune, and beyond that dune Anna had to assume there were only more dunes. The bow of the ship was pitching almost beyond her control when she had a sudden idea.

Bolting out of her captain's chair, she drew her sword, a slender rapier. She jabbed it quickly between the underside of the seat cushions and the controls, using it to wedge them into place, then darted back into the hull. The Sky-Lion's water weight had to be redistributed towards the stern, and fast, or else she would collide with the dune and likely be ripped to shreds.

Captain Anna put both hands on the lift controls that operated the ship's heavy suction valve. Steam poured out from the sides of the craft as she slowly began to crank the gear. With each turn it became a little easier until, finally, she noticed the Sky-Lion pitching upward again.

"Bingo!" she said at the success, and grabbed a rope swinging from the sail. As she wound her hand in the rope, she leaned over the port side to check how close she was to the dune—only seconds away from direct impact. With her other hand along the port balcony banister, she ran full speed up the inclined deck of the ship. She just barely made it to her seat when the ship collided with the dune.

A mighty puff and explosion of sand and debris followed. The Sky-Lion's metal underbelly screeched against the rocks in the sandy terrain, bouncing the ship hard as it skidded across the top of the sand.

Not able to hold on at impact, Captain Anna had been thrown—and rolled—all the way to the bow of the ship. She slammed into the banister along the edge and flipped over backward, leaving her dangling by her fingertips. As the Sky-Lion finally came to a rest, she held her breath to wait for the dust to settle as the creaking sounds of the airship quieted.

At last, when it seemed still, she let out a relieved sigh and blew a stray hair out of her face. She looked up to her hands as she clutched the railing, her knuckles white. She smiled at the thought of having one more story to tell about evading certain death.

But, there was no time to think about bragging now. With a grunt, she began to slowly pull herself back aboard. When she managed to get her upper body over the top of the banister, she noticed the ship was precariously perched atop the sand dune—which she knew now, was more of a cliff than a dune. Rather than skidding to a stop on its slope, as she wanted, she had inadvertently balanced the Sky-Lion over the precipice like a seesaw, ready to fall over the edge at any moment.

But she wouldn't give up.

Determined, she stood near the ship's bow and looked over the front edge. She had to gulp down her fear—the drop was at least a hundred feet onto more rocky sand. The smart thing to do would be to abandon ship, to let the vessel go. But that only left one option, jumping off the port side, and, hopefully, walking to safety or civilization before dying of thirst in the desert—she couldn't do that. She was Captain Anna Tomahawk, the greatest pilot there ever was. She could never abandon her precious Sky-Lion. Anna would rather crash with her than let her go down empty.

She had to come up with a plan, but first, she needed to get her sword back. Anna took each step with exaggerated slowness; setting her foot down timidly and grimacing as she hoped her movement wouldn't shake the ship from its perch. She walked the sloped deck to her captain's chair, where she had wedged the sword. In the crash it had become deeply lodged into the wooden steering wheel.

She looked at it and scrunched her face, slightly irritated.

"Not a problem," she said and spit into her hands, rubbing them together. She grabbed the hilt of her sword, pulling straight up. It didn't move. She yanked to either side, not even a budge. Forgetting how precariously the Sky-Lion was perched, she began to wiggle her sword back and forth as fast as she could.

The Sky-Lion bounced up and down under her forceful movement. Finally, she had had enough. She leaned against the back of her chair and put her feet up on the steering wheel. With the hilt of the sword sticking up between her knees, she yanked it as hard as she could. It popped free as the momentum from her pull swung it over her head, lodging the blade yet again into the back of the seat—and barely missing her head. Anna grunted and spun around in her seat, again wiggling the sword to get it free.

Then she noticed. All the movement and bouncing had wiggled the Sky-Lion too. She was sliding towards a devastating fall. Captain Anna took a step towards the bow to see closer, and the ship slid a little more. Another step, another foot of sliding.

She paused to think. If she went forward her weight would cause the Sky-Lion to slide off the edge. If she went back, she would have to abandon the ship and walk the desert. Anna looked around for another option, but there was nowhere else she could go.

Exasperated, she let out a sigh and dropped her shoulders. It was too much. The Sky-Lion lurched forward as the weight of the ship began to slowly pull it over the edge of the cliff.

Sometimes, at certain dire moments people instinctively know when to give up the fight and when to instead hang on for their lives. This was one of those moments. The grating screech of the Sky-Lion's metal surfaces scraping against the rock was an alarm signal to the young captain.

Time to brace for impact.

Anna leapt back towards her chair and gripped the armrests as best she could.

The Sky-Lion plummeted over the edge. As it crashed noisily into the ground it was engulfed in a giant cloud of sand and dust.

***

Maximilian Howl saw the puff of sand appear on the horizon. His eyes were accustomed to the sand. He was a desert coyote and knew the ins and outs of all of Highsand Desert. He knew where each dune started and stopped, where every cave and cactus stood, and most importantly of all he knew where each and every oasis was.

Not that there were a lot of them to keep track of.

Water was the primary commodity of Highsand. Not only because water in a desert is precious, but also because nearly all the technology in Highsand utilized steam as its power source. In truth, there was more than enough water for all the inhabitants. The trouble was King Adax owned all of it—every oasis, every puddle, every drop. Some people try to do good for others, and some try to do good for themselves. King Adax was the latter. And so he built an army to protect *his water*.

Maximilian, of course, was a scout, a royal scout actually. And he was tasked with scouring the entire desert to make sure no intruders or troublemakers showed up in King Adax's desert.

Knowing the landscape was his job and he was good at it. He was a survivor through and through. And he knew that from the distance he estimated the sand cloud plumed, something had happened at Bertha, one of the highest cliff-dunes in Highsand. It also happened to be a lookout spot that the coyote frequently used.

Whatever had happened, Maximilian knew when he heard the clatter and crashing sounds that he had to check it out right away. His canine hearing was part of what made him an excellent scout. He slung his pack and dagger onto his back and dropped onto all fours as he raced toward Bertha.

It was late in the afternoon, and it wasn't long before Maximilian was slowing down. The sand, presumably from the landslide that must have happened, was blowing down-wind and now almost totally stopping his progress toward the great cliff. When the sun finally set, he was still miles away from Bertha and still had no idea what had caused the noise and the small, but significant enough, sandstorm.

The coyote settled down against a boulder to wait out the sandstorm and began mumbling. It wasn't unusual for the scout to talk to himself out alone on the dunes.

Meanwhile, Captain Anna Tomahawk was crawling out from the wreckage of the Sky-Lion. Her pants had torn, exposing a bright red cut across her left thigh and her right boot had been pinched between some of the mangled metal in the crash, nearly tearing the sole off clean. But otherwise she was unharmed. Her sword was intact, her jacket was intact, and, thankfully, her canteen was intact.

However, the Sky-Lion was not.

She couldn't quite assess how much damage the airship had sustained with the limited light. The sun had set on the other side of the cliff, casting a dark shadow over her and the crash-site. But even in the dark she knew it wasn't flyable.

Watching that her arms and legs didn't get cut against the many pieces of jagged metal and splintered wooden beams, she searched through the wreck, collected the supplies she could carry in her leather bag, and headed east, the direction she had previously been flying. The brave captain hadn't gone far before she heard a clear voice coming across the desert. It had a strange accent that the girl had never heard before. Yet, it was a pleasant accent, and she found what it was saying quite humorous. As she got closer, she began to identify the creature's form.

"Oh, hello, I didn't see you there."

At first Anna thought she had been spotted, but it turned out the wolf was talking to himself. She stayed quiet and watched from a distance.

"You shouldn't be sneaking around; not acceptable on my sand dunes. Not acceptable at all. Oh, what's that? You've got a mouth on you huh? Well, perhaps I can teach you some manners with my sword! On-guard!"

She looked on as the wolf drew a short, glimmering dagger and started dueling with an imaginary foe. Weaving up and down with his weapon swiftly, although, Anna noted, with little skill.

"You're quite good with a sword, you scoundrel! But I'm General Maximilian Howl, and you're no match for me!" And with a final fierce stab he shouted, "Ha!" and vanquished his pretend enemy, quickly sheathing the dagger and turning away.

"Who are you talking to?" Anna asked innocently as she emerged from the dusty, night air.

"Ha-Howl! On-guard!" Maximilian, taken by surprise, turned around again, drawing his weapon.

Captain Anna smiled. "I don't think you want to fight with me, Mr. Wolf."

"Wolf? I'm a coyote."

"Right, well, whatever you are—you don't want to duel me."

"You're trespassing in the Highsand Desert; and as you know, no one trespasses unless...unless King Adax says they can trespass!" Maximilian reached back and grabbed his lantern from a rock. He stepped closer, holding up the light to identify his new, and much more real, rival.

"Actually, I don't know," the fearless captain replied coolly, "and I didn't mean to upset you, Your Highness." She took a low exaggerated bow.

"I'm not...I'm not King Adax! I'm Maximilian Howl, servant of the king. And I'm in charge of these dunes, bit of an enforcer if you catch my wind." The coyote scratched under his chin with the back of a claw, "Not many people don't know who King Adax is...who are you anyway?"

"You don't know who *I* am?" she asked, her mouth hanging open in surprise. "Come on, don't you recognize me? Hold on." Captain Anna Tomahawk struck a heroic pose, and trying not to ruin her stance spoke with barely moving her lips, "How about now?"

He shrugged.

She twitched her nose at his lack of recognition. "No, huh? I can't believe it. I'm world famous, you know. If you'll permit me to honor you with my grandeur," she gestured toward his dagger with her eyes and a nod.

Maximilian reluctantly sheathed his weapon.

"I'll give you some hints. I am the greatest explorer there ever was!" She talked a little too loud, too excited. "Captain of the Sky-Lion, the greatest airship there ever was! Traveling fair and fierce skies of every land! Number one swashbuckling, pistol-wielding wonder known to both man and beast as a," she searched for the right word, "a threat. Hero," she drummed on her chest twice, "that's what they call me."

"Hmmm."

"You don't believe me?"

Maximilian just stared. One gray bushy eyebrow rose in suspicion.

"Well, look, right over there is my ship the Sky-Lion, best airship ever built!" Maximilian squinted into the desert night, not seeing anything. "Well, it's just back that way," she said, forgetting that she had walked a few miles.

Maximilian half-turned, keeping an eye on the girl, and went to his pack. After a moment he produced a pair of binoculars with green lenses and leather straps hanging down from the corners. He held them up to his eyes. "Looks like a piece of junk to me."

"Well, it's the best. At least, it used to be before I just crashed. Captain Anna Tomahawk," she extended her hand, "Pleased to meet you Max."

"I prefer Maximilian...Captain." Maximilian was admittedly impressed by her airship, wrecked or not, and her exuberant confidence.

She shook his paw vigorously. "Sure, okay. Well, I'm going to need some parts if I'm to sail again. You can't see it from here, but my thruster pipes are melted and my dorsal blades are torn. The starboard side wing blade is completely ripped off, not to mention the hull damage from the two crashes and the *missile* that took me down."

Maximilian, confused by her technical jargon, struggled for the words to respond. "Forgive me, Captain, did you say *missile*?"

"Yep, just over that large dune, that way. I can't imagine who would shoot at *me*. I've never been this far out before. No enemies here I know of." Captain Anna gave him a wink.

"Yes, well, I think King Adax would be most interested to meet you."

"Would he be able to help fix the Sky-Lion?"

"Able to?" Maximilian chuckled. "Yes, he's a person of great...resources, shall we say."

"Is that him on your cloak?" Captain Anna asked, pointing to the scorpion insignia on Maximilian's shoulder.

"This? King Adax?" Maximilian laughed again. "No. This is his symbol. It's how he marks his things. He's a beetle. A dung beetle, actually. I'm sure he'd like to be a scorpion."

"I don't know why anyone would want to be a scorpion—even a beetle. My symbol is way better anyway. Want to see it?"

"Hmm," Maximilian grunted. He was indeed curious, but trying not to show it. Any symbol other than the one of King Adax was a sight to see.

Anna dropped her pack on the ground behind her and, turning her back to the coyote, began digging through its contents. Maximilian noted how she turned her back to him, as if she didn't have a fear in the world. As she searched through the large bag, she flung the contents over her shoulder, a canteen, a tomahawk, a hat, some goggles, and finally, she pulled out the flag. She drew it out in a great arch with a flourish and a dainty spin. The kind only girls, like Captain Anna, know quite how to perform. "This is it!" She displayed for Maximilian a bright blue flag, its centerpiece a dark green leaf.

Maximilian, took a step towards the flag and the girl, lantern raised, eyes getting wide, "Is that a leaf?"

"Yep," said the young captain, noticing the puzzled reaction of the coyote. "Why's that so special?"

"Astonishing," Maximilian said in wonder, feeling the cloth with his paw. He nearly fell into a trance looking at it. "Sorry," he said, shaking his snout after a moment, "it has just been a very long time since I've seen a leaf is all."

"Oh, well, maybe once the Sky-Lion is fixed you could come back with me; there are *tons* of leaves where I'm from."

"Where did you say you came from?"

"Well, I was actually on my way home from a great world traveling expedition. I was looking for this." She pulled out a ruby pendant hanging from her neck by a leather strap. "Getting it back was quite an adventure, and very dangerous," Anna shook her finger at Maximilian. "Then there was a crazy storm and the Sky-Lion was rocking back and forth, so I had to land on an island, and I met this monkey named Maurice who was sad all the time, but not any more 'cause we're friends now, and I ate a coconut."

"I see." Maximilian couldn't believe his eyes and ears. As preposterous as it all was, this girl wasn't from Highsand. She was an outsider! "And now you're here?"

"Exactomundo, now I'm here," Anna looked around, "in the desert." She brushed some sand off her jacket sleeve.

"King Adax will be most interested in you indeed."

"Oh, good, I'm excited to meet him! Shall we be off then, Max?"

"Maximilian."

"Right. Maximilian."

Anna began restocking her bag with the strewn contents, when Maximilian finally recognized what it was she was holding. He stopped her with his sharp tone, "Is that a canteen?"

"Yep," her answer polite.

"With water?" Maximilian asked incredulously.

"Yeah, do you want some?"

"Where did you get it?"

"Well, the canteen used to be my father's, and—"

"No, the water," his tone was impatient.

"Oh, um, the river." Captain Anna responded to Maximilian's inquiries with a genuine naivety. In her world travels she had come across many places, but none so different as Highsand Desert. Greatest captain and swashbuckler or not, she could hardly have been prepared for the adventure she was beginning.

All Maximilian could say was how very interesting it was indeed.

CHAPTER 2

That same night and not too far away from Anna and Maximilian's campsite, King Adax sat on his throne. He was sipping on a drink out of a big yellow, gold chalice held in one of his four beetle hands; his hard beetle shell seemed to frame the crown of jewels that adorned his scaly head, and his beetle antennae and horn stuck out of the top of the crown in a grotesque display of his mighty beetletude. Along with his dominating physical presence, his demeanor this evening was somewhat perturbed.

Sheena, his number one assistant and an old woman whose wrinkles were only outnumbered by her bad moods, was giving him updates on various affairs of his empire. She was a suck up and she was always trying to impress King Adax with her unimpeachable foulness, which was of course, the one thing King Adax liked—being bad.

"There was another disruption at the wells today," Sheena said. "The soldiers arrested a number of *troublemakers* that will need to be questioned."

King Adax was tired, not to mention that he was on a backswing from an earlier outburst of anger, "Oh," he groaned in his sand-paper voice, "not now Sheena, I wanted—"

"We shot down an enemy ship, Sire!" cried Burp, crashing into the throne room through the high-arched double doors, which slammed into the walls behind their hinges with a bang.

"I shot it down, you fool!" Belch scolded at his partner. Both hedgehogs, more hog than hedge, had a talent for bickering amongst themselves. "Burp was only watching, Your Majesty!"

"I spotted it flying, Belch, and you know it!"

"Well, I still shot it down!" They quickly burst into a series of objections against one another, their volume increasing as their words became less intelligible.

"Enough!" shouted King Adax, loud enough to make even Sheena tremble. The twin hedgehogs, Burp and Belch, twitched their noses and pricked up, literally. "What ship? What are you two idiots talking about?" King Adax's temper was flaring.

"Your Majesty," Burp started, bowing low and catching his breath, "I spotted a ship flying over Highsand Desert. An airship. Small craft, crew-size unidentified—"

"An airship! How?" How, indeed, was the most pressing question. Airships were unheard of in

Highsand. Kind Adax had strictly outlawed any construction of flying crafts under a law that prevented overuse of water for any *extraneous purposes*. Not that anyone knew how to build an airship anyway. Still, it was the king's most important law, and he imposed it with great prejudice. "Where did it come from? What was on it?" The king's patience was depleted, his mind in an unusual panic.

"We don't know yet, Your Majesty." Burp said.

"I shot it out of the sky, just a moment ago." Belch cut in, "We used the ballista we built last week. Quite effective at a distance, as we hoped."

Burp and Belch, though obnoxious and oftentimes absent minded, were the best engineers in Highsand, able to construct almost anything out of the limited desert materials. Almost. The one thing they could never build was, in fact, an airship. The technology, though permitted to them as an exception to the king's law, was out of their grasp.

"Well, what are you doing here? The intruders could have already escaped, you blithering idiots! No one is allowed to fly. Go find the wreckage and bring me back whoever and whatever you find."

"Aye-aye!" the hedgehogs shouted in unison. With a salute they turned quickly to exit, tripping over one another the whole way.

Sheena begrudgingly walked over to the throne room doors and pushed each one shut with much chagrin. As she turned back to the king, her shoulders relaxed. Knowing they were alone put her at ease. "Those two will never find anything in the desert," she said, "not with their eyesight, and not with their bickering."

"I know that. That's why we have Maximilian." King Adax let out an exasperated grunt, "Hopefully, he's already come across the vessel."

"An airship could be very dangerous." Sheena tended to remind King Adax of things he already knew. "If anyone in Highsand could get into the air, they could discover the jungle isn't as far as we would have them believe," she said in a low voice.

King Adax took a slow breath, for he and Sheena were keepers of a great secret. Though he longed to forget it, Adax knew of the jungle. If he could, he would erase all knowledge and memory of it. He resented the jungle and all who lived there. The mighty dung beetle had long ago been exiled to Highsand as punishment for crimes against the king of the jungle. He and hundreds of others with him, all the worst of criminals, had been banished. Sentenced to live out their days in the desert.

Over years of fighting amongst themselves and struggling to build a civilization out of the dust, the violent and treacherous group had one by one fallen as Adax gained power.

He grew stronger in the desert. He used his natural abilities and cunning to push out and defeat all his opponents, declaring himself king. He built his empire from blood and sand. Those who refused to join him were killed. Those who attempted to leave were killed. Everyone who was willing to serve the beetle was forced to forget the stories of the past. The jungle faded from the memory of all the people of Highsand until it was nothing but a myth.

What had once been known as true became a fable that only the brave or insane would dare utter.

Now, the only ones still alive who knew the truth were the king himself and Sheena, his oldest and most ruthlessly loyal servant.

Indeed, although Highsand Desert was the largest, most dangerous, dry, discouraging empire of sand known anywhere, King Adax's palace and his capital city—Dung Dune City—were altogether not too far from the Blue River, and therefore not too far from the jungle. But that didn't matter, because the people and animals of Dung Dune City, and all of the animals and all the people of all of Highsand, were hopelessly lost in the desert.

Still, the myths couldn't be destroyed. Couldn't be blotted out. They were too compelling, and they were too hopeful. Even after all this time there were some, even though they'd never seen it, who believed that the desert did have an edge. Hopeful dreamers. They were a small group of rebels who, reasonably enough, called themselves *the Edges*.

"Yes, yes. I know that airships are dangerous," King Adax severed Sheena's thought process with his own. "We'll be in luck if whoever was on-board was killed in the crash. If they weren't they mustn't be allowed to spread word of the outside." King Adax's voice held some nervousness that Sheena had not heard before.

"Your Majesty, what if the rebels find the wreck before Maximilian does? They could possibly gain support from within the city. There could be an uproar, rioting."

King Adax's anger was building and he spoke through a clenched jaw, "Well, if Maximilian lets any survivors escape, his fur will cover my new throne cushion!" He slammed all four of his fists down on his armrests. The sound of his exoskeleton on the hard metal echoed through the chamber.

Sheena let the sound sink into the walls as the room faded into eerie silence. "Of course, Your Majesty." Sheena said, trying to reassure and calm him.

"Here's what will happen," King Adax seemed to threaten a prophecy. "Maximilian will find the airship and bury it. He will capture whoever is still alive and bring them back to the palace. We will interrogate and, if necessary, *eliminate them*. We must make absolutely certain that no one hears any wonder stories about some jungle paradise. We've gone through too much to let the stories of green, growing things resurface," he said with disgust. "Oceans of water as far as the eye can see—no, if they want water, they come to me. Who built a kingdom out of loose sand? Who forced the lazy and weak to build walls that provided shelter from the sandstorms? Who built an army and an empire out of nothing, asking only for *volunteers*? I did. I did! I distribute the water and the food as I see fit and all I ask for is loyalty. I won't have some stranger flying in on an airship ruining it with rumors and lies of better lands. The jungle doesn't exist! There is no edge to my kingdom. No one has ever come to Highsand before, and no one ever will. For the sake of my empire this secret must be kept."

"How?" Sheena asked.

"We take the airship for ourselves." King Adax's mind was reeling with anger and terror at what the presence of a flying vessel could do to his power.

"What would we do with an airship?"

"Discover its secrets. Go to war."

"But, Your Majesty, if you send an army into the jungle, they'll abandon your cause when they see the prosperity. You can't fight the jungle cities." Sheena quickly realized she had put her foot in her mouth when King Adax stood from his throne and in a seemingly single movement traversed half the room.

"Are my subjects not loyal!?" the king roared, towering over his advisor.

"Your Majesty, forgive me, what I meant was that the people, some of the people are...ungrateful for your kindness."

"Then perhaps there is another way. If I can't send an army, perhaps I can fight them myself. Who is stronger than me?"

"I don't understand," said Sheena.

"What if I had my own airship? A warship."

"A warship," she repeated.

"Yes. The biggest, most powerful airship ever built. With it I could burn the jungle to the ground, pour flaming oil from the air upon every city in the jungle. Then there would be no place to go but to me. The jungle will cease to exist, just as we have strived to accomplish for all these years. I'll burn and pulverize everything until ash and dust and sand cover the world. The desert will stretch out its hands and blot out the putrid, green, growing forests. I will drink the oceans and rivers dry, and I will become king of everything because everything...will be desert." His plan was equal parts evil and raving mad.

"King Adax," Sheena stepped back, her wrinkled eyes peering up at the beetle's shining and evil physiognomy, "King Adax, we," she was stammering in fear, "we don't know how to build an airship."

"No, we don't," he said ominously, "but maybe our new guests will."

***

Burp and Belch, having been given their instructions, set off immediately to their lab. Being hedgehogs, they were, like many animals and people in Highsand, not naturally adept in the desert. Furthermore, since they lived relative lives of comfort in service of the king, they had little need to adapt to the conditions outside Dung Dune City. So for traveling instances such as this, they had constructed an all-terrain—which in Highsand is really only sandy terrain—vehicle that they proudly named the Worm.

After some arguing about what to bring with them, they decided it was best to stick with only the essentials—their pistols and sand goggles. Burp and Belch were always up to no good. So, in order to keep their scheming projects secretive, they always left and reentered the city by a secret tunnel. A tunnel that King Adax had dug personally—being a giant dung beetle did have some advantages.

As the exterior gate at the far end of the dark tunnel opened, a rush of sand and hot, dry desert air swept into the tunnel—an expected nuisance. Sand drifts often covered outward facing walls and smaller side entrances alike, nearly burying the city alive.

The two hedgehogs coughed through the sand cloud as the Worm's noisy engine clanked and plowed heavily through the entrance. It was past midnight, and the hot sun had not risen. Still, they could make out a fading cloud of smoke high up in the distant, night sky. It would likely vanish in a few hours, but all they needed was a general direction. They'd find their way eventually.

"Turn left!" Belch shouted.

"No, turn right!" Burp countered, and so they began their weaving and unpredictable route to the crash site of the Sky-Lion.

High upon the Worm's back sat a cage of barbed rails for any prisoners they might capture at the crash site, the metal spikes glimmering in the light from the lanterns that covered the Worm.

CHapTeR 3

Maximilian looked over his shoulder towards the young captain; she'd unbuttoned her bright red jacket to expose a white tank top that glinted in the moonlight. It seemed brighter against the backdrop of the desert sand, which was reflecting the moonlight with an eerie, blue glow. She was a walking beacon. Maximilian could see the weary look in her young face. "It's just twenty-six more dunes that way. We'll be there by morning; come on now."

"Max, we've been walking for hours! Don't you think we could stop for the night somewhere? Aren't there any trees or shelter out here?"

"Trees? Hardly. Maybe a cactus if King Adax hasn't had it cut down already. But mostly there's no shelter. Only the strongest survive out here in the desert." Maximilian was still not sure if Anna was, in fact, *"the greatest airship pilot to ever live"* or any of the other lofty things she claimed to be.

Trust was not something Maximilian Howl gave out easily, and especially not to such a young girl making such grandiose claims.

"Of course," Anna said, "only the strongest survive. But let's clear something up, shall we? Since I'm a Captain, and you're a Scout, I think I outrank you. Don't I?"

Maximilian was caught off-guard, "Well, well, not in the traditional—"

"Let's say, that for the rest of the night, you know, until we can get it totally squared away, I'm in charge. And I say, we camp." Anna struck one of her many heroic poses. She stood with her hands planted on her hips pushing out her chest and throwing back her shoulders.

Maximilian had to admit it was a very impressive stance. "Fine," he grumbled out. "But at first light we will be off." And without another word Maximilian trotted a few quick circles, as canines typically do before settling in, and dropped into the sand. A small puff of dust fanned around him.

"Wait, you don't have a tent or anything?" Anna had expected better accommodations than sleeping in the open desert air.

"I'm a coyote. We don't use tents. We're tough, crafty." Maximilian rolled back over dismissively.

Anna waited a few moments to see if anything further was coming from the coyote. When it didn't, her desire to stay up and talk grew almost unbearable. Anna always had trouble sleeping when she knew an adventure was right around the corner.

Keeping Maximilian from his sleep, she started again, "Oh, I didn't realize you were such a crafty coyote."

Maximilian rolled over once more, trying to ignore her. "Well, I am." He shut his eyes for the third time.

Anna waited for a few moments. The temperature was dropping and the wind was picking up. Now that they had stopped walking, she was beginning to get cold. With the rip in the thigh of her pants and the laceration that came with it, it was hard to stay covered. Her body heat was escaping through her wound. Even with her jacket buttoned and the collar flipped high around her neck she was starting to shiver.

Not having any desert experience, Captain Tomahawk looked to Maximilian as the example of proper sand-country etiquette. She mimicked his positioning by walking a few quick circles and plopping down into as tiny of a ball as she could.

It didn't help.

The wind was biting at her lower back where the jacket didn't quite reach to cover. Not knowing what else to do, she slowly started creeping over towards the coyote.

"Achoo!"

Maximilian didn't move.

She cleared her throat and continued, "Ahem, achoo! Burrrrrr! Ahem, Burrrrr!"

Maximilian, having been listening to her fake sneezes and whimpers for the past few minutes, finally turned to her bothered. "Yes?" He licked his front teeth in frustration.

"Oh, you're awake too?"

Captain Anna's plan did not involve much beyond getting Maximilian's attention, but it was certainly better to have company if she was going to be cold. "Too bad we don't have any wood to start a fire. It's awfully cold once the sun goes down."

Maximilian twitched his nose, annoyed that after all her talk of stopping to set camp the young, girl captain wouldn't even attempt falling asleep. "I hadn't noticed. Mother always said I had the thickest fur she'd ever seen on a coyote."

"Well, since you can't tell, I'll inform you: it's cold."

Maximilian wasn't without a heart, and as bothersome as Anna's childlike behavior was at the moment, he had to admit he liked her pluck and spirit.

"How about this? You can have my cape…for now." Standing, Maximilian took off his red cape and wrapped it gently around the girl. He placed his paw briefly over the royal insignia as he finished draping it around her shoulders.

It was during this exact moment of movement and rustle that three characters began edging their way down the dune behind them, quietly and carefully.

"Thank you, Max!" Anna perked up. "You're quite the gentleman…with a little coaxing." She winked at him.

Maximilian looked her over as he scratched his neck, wondering if he'd been played. "That's Maximilian, and thank you. I think."

Captain Anna hummed with new warmth. "I like your cape, it's warm. And it makes me feel like a soldier!" She twirled, spinning the cape out.

"But you're a Captain, aren't you?"

"Yes," Anna said defensively, "but not a soldiering captain. I'm a giving orders kind of captain."

"You don't seem very commanding," Maximilian said with a smirk.

"I have my moments." As the words came out of her mouth she saw them—and barely soon enough. Three strangers sprung upon their makeshift camp. Maximilian jumped up and drew his dagger. Anna instinctively went back-to-back with him, but kept her sword buckled in its sheath. Maximilian, living up to his name, let out a sharp, angry howl.

"Halt!" Shouted the tallest of the invading group. He was wearing a wide brimmed hat and had a long, yellow beard. His right leg was entirely mechanical from the knee down. He reached for a wingnut attached to a bolt on the top of his knee. Steam hissed out as he visibly became more comfortable. "We meet again, Maximilian!"

"Lieutenant Larraby! I should've known you'd find me if I stopped moving long enough."

Larraby's eyes flared with anger. "You've been a nightmare to catch, you no-good steamin' traitor!"

"Max isn't a traitor!" Anna declared with conviction.

"Quiet, little girl! This is a conversation for adults and coyotes only. Apple, keep her quiet!"

"Yes, sir!" said Apple, one of Lieutenant Larraby's henchmen. Before she could react, he brought a dagger up to Anna's tender throat and twisted her away from her defensive huddle with Maximilian. She swallowed her next protest as the blade pressed against her skin.

"Don't touch her!" Maximilian roared, furious, "That's *my* prisoner!"

"Prisoner?" Anna thought aloud, looking at Maximilian for an explanation. He didn't even glance at her.

"No talking," said Apple as he pressed the sharp knife into her neck, drawing a red bead of blood. Anna strained away from the knife with a grimace.

"She doesn't look like a prisoner to me, Maximilian—not in that cape." Lieutenant Larraby's golden beard and mustache were caked with sand, and as he spoke, dust drifted away from his face.

"She's staying with *me*." Maximilian pressed.

"Well, then she's coming with *us*. You're going to face consequences for betraying the free people to King Adax." Larraby spit, "You know how many were lost to the desert once you gave away the position of our base!"

"I had no choice," Maximilian said, dropping his head and eyes.

"There's always a choice, Maximilian. And you chose wrong."

"It wasn't that simple, Larraby."

"It doesn't matter, you're coming with us, and we'll bury you alive. The same punishment your *king* had for our people." Larraby twisted his face into a snarl.

Anna was utterly lost, *what were they talking about?* But, she noticed that Apple, the clumsy henchman, was also focused on Maximilian and Larraby's dialogue.

She sensed an opportunity.

Anna slipped her hand around her belt, making sure to not alert Apple, whose arms were wrapped around her tightly. She could barely reach the trigger of her pistol with the tip of her finger, but using her hip to angle the shot, she was able to squeeze off a single round.

As the hammer clapped down, the sound of exploding gunpowder was replaced by the wailing of Apple. The one-chance-shot had gone clean through the toe of his boot. The moment his arms flew up Anna shoved him away from her with a swift elbow and drew her slender sword violently from her other hip.

"Max is staying with me!" she said as she leapt towards the other two invaders.

In the confusion of the gunshot and the screaming, Larraby, Max, and the other henchman were still trying to figure out what had happened. The pause was more than enough time for Anna to make her move, sword out in front.

Larraby stepped back on his metal leg as Apple's screams slowly faded into groans. He could hear Apple saying, "She shot me! That little girl shot me!"

"What is this, Maximilian?" Larraby wasn't about to cower to a little girl, gun or not. "Your steamin' prisoner coming to your rescue?"

"I'm not a prisoner. Tell him, Max." Anna waited, but Maximilian didn't respond.

He just stared at Larraby hard.

Thinking Maximilian was too afraid to help she started again, "I'm Captain Anna Tomahawk of the Sky-Lion, and I'm the meanest-dueling, quickest-shooting *pilot* there ever was. I can shoot a match head off a stick from a mile away with my eyes closed. And I'm giving you one chance, right now, to surrender!"

If there was one thing Anna was truly excellent at, it was showing off.

"Hard to believe all those claims from such a small girl!" said Larraby, not impressed by her bragging. Ignoring any apprehension her age might have given him, Larraby suddenly swung his sword and sprung at Anna with a thrust.

Anna saw it coming.

She sidestepped the attack and countered by kicking the lieutenant behind his good knee. He stumbled forward only to regain his balance and spin on her with another thrust of his sword. Anna parried the blow and lashed out with her own blade. She jumped and swung high. But the swordsman ducked under it—just in time for the swipe to sheer through the edge of his wide-brimmed hat.

Being small and nimble rather than large and clumsy had some advantages in a sword fight, but even with a heavy mechanical leg to slow him down, the lieutenant's arms were twice as long as the young captain's. She would have to be in a dangerously close zone in order to land a blow. Larraby, in frustration, had gone from finesse to berserk and was slashing his sword wildly in a giant X, pushing Anna up the side of a sand hill. Anna knew she couldn't keep up her back-pedaling much longer.

She looked down to his leg and saw a small steam gauge, indicating that his leg was about to overheat. It was the same type of gauge that she used on the Sky-Lion.

With her free hand she reached down to her pistol and drew it up. The barrel aligned right between Larraby's eyes.

He paused.

It was just a moment's hesitation in his feverish onslaught, but it was long enough. Anna thrust her sword down the side of Larraby's blade, and with some ear-piercing, metal-on-metal grating she stabbed it into the hilt of Larraby's sword.

It locked them together. Anna leaned into the attack on Larraby's right side, putting as much weight as she could on his mechanical leg. He cried out in pain as the valve overheated and sent steam shooting from the top of his clockwork knee.

As the bearded assailant's attention shifted to his leg, Anna took the opportunity to lodge her sword further between the metal spokes of Larraby's cross-guard. She began to twist, and with a few brilliant flourishes and arcs of her arm, she sent his sword flying into the air. It landed twenty feet away, piercing the sand and wobbling back and forth in the ground. She kept both her gun and sword pointed directly at him.

Lieutenant Larraby made a brief, hesitant move toward his lost weapon. "You can leave that there, Mister," said Anna, threatening him with her sword. "And you should probably help your friend," she motioned with her head towards Apple. In the commotion, Anna hadn't noticed that Maximilian had managed to defeat the third henchman, who was now limping away in the moonlight.

"This won't be the last you see of me, Maximilian," Larraby growled, realizing his defeat. "And as for you, you don't know what kind of company you carry. You should go home, girl."

"That's exactly what I'm trying to do," Anna's eyes narrowed.

Maximilian and Anna stood for a few moments in total silence, well, except for their panting, of which Anna's sounded nearly as dog-like as Maximilian's. They watched the three men struggle off into the desert night. Anna's fighting personality, Maximilian noted, was nearly the opposite of her natural girl-child demeanor. She was still as sure and confident as ever, but in a very different way.

Maximilian had been thinking this very thing when Anna said, "Whew! That was close!" Her naivety and happy disposition returning quickly, accompanied by her precocious smile. She contorted her lips to blow her hair out of her face.

"Close?" Maximilian balked. "That was amazing, Captain! How'd you escape from the henchman?"

Captain Anna shrugged.

"Amazing!" Maximilian said excited. "You really *are* the greatest in the world, aren't you?"

"I'm not a liar, Max," Anna said seriously, sheathing her sword and plunging her pistol back into its holster with a spin.

"You saved my life." Maximilian looked up at her.

Anna cracked a smile, "I'm a hero. It's what I do."

"Of course, of course." Maximilian shook his head, still dumbfounded by her skill. "We'd better be off. Best not to wait for them to come back." Maximilian looked in all directions, his eyes shaking nervously.

"First," Anna stopped him, "what was all that about me being your prisoner? As I recall, I'm in charge." Anna gave a broad smile; seemingly totally oblivious to the palpable manipulation she was under.

"It was nothing, just a trick," Maximilian offered as a defense. "A ruse, a coyote being crafty."

Anna gave the crafty coyote a quizzical look, and then, deciding he was being honest, agreed. "Hmm. If you say so," and she shrugged again. "But who were those guys?"

Maximilian stooped to pick up Larraby's sword, "Do you want it?"

"It's yours now," she said. "A real sword will be *way* better than that little dagger." Anna giggled to his embarrassment.

Maximilian slipped the sword through a spare loop in his belt, "They were…rebels. They don't like the king."

"Why not?"

Maximilian sighed. "Probably lots of reasons."

Maximilian and Anna stared at one another for a moment. Maximilian couldn't tell if the young captain was reading into his words, if he should've been more selective in his discourse.

"Now, let's get moving. I want to be in the palace by morning. We can rest when we arrive."

"But, they called you a *traitor*, Max! That's terrible!"

"Yes. It's a long story—*for another time*. We need to get moving." Maximilian knew that it was likely the king would send someone out looking for the airship and its crew, and he wanted to personally be the one to bring Anna in. It might put him back into the temperamental beetle's favor.

"Mind if I keep the cape on?" Anna twirled peacefully as she had before.

"Not at all, you look pretty in red, young Captain."

"Thank you, Max," she said in a polite tone. "When I grow up, I think I'll add 'the most *beautiful* pilot in the world' to my title."

"If you grow up." Maximilian mumbled.

"What?"

"Nothing, it would be a suitable name for you." Maximilian's whiskers twitched.

Chapter 4

"I told you it was this way," Burp scolded as the Worm grinded to a halt, black smoke billowing out of its sides. The Worm was at the base of Bertha. Below its cockpit, where Burp and Belch sat, was the wreckage of the Sky-Lion.

"Fine, you were right," Belch conceded, "Let's check it out."

The two hedgehogs climbed down the front of the Worm with skill and obvious experience. Most noteworthy to the engineers was the size of the craft, only enough room for a handful of a crew at most. They took measurements of the deck and wings, and knowing nothing about flying ships, they made incorrect assumptions everywhere they looked. They were trying to convince one another that they did indeed know what each and every part of the ship was and did. The one thing they did identify accurately was the blasted starboard-side wing.

"It was a great shot, Belch."

"Nice of you to finally admit it," Belch said proudly, his quills spreading in a fan.

"Should we drag it aboard the Worm and bring it back to the lab? Or just bury it here?" Burp asked.

"Let's bring it back. King Adax will want to see it."

"Without a crew? He'll want to know why we didn't find any crew. Or bodies," Burp said, shaking with a chill of worry.

As if charged by the same idea, the two hedgehogs scampered back up the Worm and put their goggles on. The green lenses blinked to life as they cranked the gears on either side of the goggles' straps. The goggles were one of the few more sophisticated technologies they had that didn't run on water. With them the hedgehogs could see much better in the dark, and could hope to identify any crawling survivors in the nearby sand. They spun in circles, scanning the area.

"Nothing," said Belch.

"Nothing," said Burp. "Get the chain."

Belch disappeared into the hull of the Worm and, finding the correct crank, pulled and kicked until it finally heaved around its rotation. The maw on the Worm's front opened wide as a bolted chain shot out with terrifying speed. It pierced right through the wooden side of the Sky-Lion, sending splinters everywhere.

With a release of another lever, hooks opened at the end of the chain, locking the Worm's grip onto the airship. Then with unnaturally loud noise, Burp and Belch worked the gears to drag the Sky-Lion right into the mouth of the Worm.

Not too far away, Lieutenant Larraby, Apple, and Truck, his other guard, heard the noise of the Sky-Lion being dragged aboard the Worm. The three turned around and took off running in that direction, Apple obviously trailing behind with his foot bleeding. He knew that he'd lost his smallest toe to Anna's pistol, but there was no time to grieve it now—he had a new sense of balance to learn.

As the three crested the top of a dune, they looked down and easily spotted the Worm. The hedgehogs had nearly every lamp on the back of the giant vehicle illuminated. They weren't much for stealth, and it showed how confident they were to defend themselves.

Larraby and Truck were lying down as flat as possible on the top of the dune. Reaching down, Larraby quietly released the pressure from the valve on his knee as he strained to see through the sandy air.

Apple was below the ridge behind them. "What do you see?" he asked.

"It's Burp and Belch," Larraby whispered, "more of King Adax's cronies. They're dragging something aboard the Worm. Cage is empty." Larraby noticed the cage atop the Worm almost immediately. He had been captured once before by Burp and Belch and carried in that very cage halfway across the desert to be executed. Only by a great deal of luck—and the hedgehogs' non-stop arguing—had he managed to escape.

"It's stuck, Burp!"

"Go shake it or something!"

Larraby could hear the two hedgehogs fighting quite clearly in the midst of the otherwise quiet desert night.

"It's too big, Burp. We'll have to break it apart or leave it here and bury it."

"I'm not going to smash it any further to bits and have the king upset about us ruining his flying ship."

His flying ship? Larraby thought. *Did I hear that right?*

"Fine. So we bury it!" Belch yelled, making an executive decision before Burp had time to officially agree. With some manipulation from the cockpit, the Worm slowly tilted its head up and then down. Belch slammed the controls to their limits, left and right. The Worm shook its head in response. The wrecked airship fell out of its grip noisily. The metal underbelly of the Sky-Lion banged into the fitted teeth of the Worm's lower jaw.

Once it had fallen totally free, Burp and Belch began to retract the chain without any precautions of silence.

Larraby and Truck slipped back down the other side of the hill towards Apple.

"We've got to get closer and investigate, Apple," Larraby said to his wounded man. "I'm going to need to send you to the base alone. Can you make it back?"

Apple gritted his teeth and nodded dutifully.

"When you arrive, send help," Larraby grasped Apple's shoulder. "We have to get that ship in our possession."

"That girl—" Apple started, but the lieutenant cut him off.

"Yes, I know."

They were all thinking it. That little girl really might have been "Captain of the Sky-Lion" as she claimed. Had she said *pilot*? Yes, it all made sense. Maximilian Howl must've come across her wrecked ship, must've been just before Larraby's scouting party had sprung upon them. But, was she an outsider? Was she from Highsand? She was wearing the king's cape and insignia, but Maximilian had called her "prisoner." Lieutenant Larraby's mind was racing.

He needed answers. But first, he had to get that ship; it was the only way to sway any power favorably towards the Edges.

For Lieutenant Larraby was, in fact, the leader of the Edges, the group of rebels that had broken away from King Adax's ruthless control. They were mostly families, animal and human; they weren't strong. They didn't have numbers, didn't have weapons hardly at all. They didn't have much of anything, really, except for a belief that the desert wasn't forever.

What they did have was hope. They hoped for rivers and green things and freedom. If Larraby could bring back an airship—a real airship—it would change everything. It would bolster the revolution. It would prove to everyone, even those still unconvinced and deceived in Dung Dune City, that there was another place not so far out of reach, where King Adax didn't control everything.

Lieutenant Larraby had to get that ship, because if an airship could exist, then so too might a place with freedom. "Go, Apple," Larraby said with inspiration, "To the edge!" and he saluted.

"And the farthest shore," Apple saluted and responded with the appropriate phrase, then without hesitation, he turned to head off towards the Edges' base.

The first oranges of dawn were beginning to show in the lowest clouds of the sky. When Larraby and Truck peaked back over the hill, Burp and Belch were already in the process of burying the Sky-Lion. Using some mechanism of the Worm to drill underneath the sand, the two hedgehogs caused a small dune collapse and the Sky-Lion sank neatly beneath the surface of the desert.

By the time the process was completely finished, the sun was rising. It was morning. Larraby had watched all through the night thinking about the significance of an airship. It could change everything for the Edges—for good or for bad.

The very moment the Worm twisted noisily around and began its rumble back to Dung Dune City, Larraby and Truck leapt over the side of the dune and slid down the sandy embankment towards the buried treasure.

Towards hope.

They both began digging with their hands and feet to uncover the ship.

***

Maximilian and Anna's night was also turning out to be an adventure. They reached Dung Dune City well before morning. Anna's fear of being caught again by Larraby and his men, and Maximilian's fear of running into more of his comrades, who might want to claim the girl as their own discovery, had kept them moving. Quickly.

They had nearly doubled their speed in order to get to the city when they did.

But upon arriving, Maximilian had a change of heart, or at least, a change of mind. The truth was, Maximilian rather liked Captain Anna Tomahawk. She had spirit and was full of energy and she was kind to him. Maximilian could hardly remember the last time someone had been kind to him. She called him a gentleman. She had saved him from being captured by Larraby, saved his life even. What kind of noble coyote would he be if he surrendered the young girl captain to an unknown end?

And it was unknown. There had never been a flying ship before. There had never been someone from beyond the desert either. He had no hint of what would happen if he took her to King Adax. What she would be made to do, or what would be done to her. What saddened Maximilian the most was the thought that she might change her mind about him—or worse, that she would be made to hate him entirely—if he turned her in to such an end.

He had to think.

Maximilian Howl was not one to act rashly. He was crafty. He was the son of intelligent coyote parents, and he was a proud strategy-making thinker. He wouldn't run head first into anything he didn't understand yet. So, instead of taking Anna directly to the palace, he decided to hide her, for a while at least, deep in the heart of Dung Dune City.

Dung Dune City was not only the most overcrowded and busy city of Highsand—maybe anywhere—but also, a city filled with crime and fear. Most of the regular citizens were afraid of King Adax's troops, who, ironically, were the most criminal element in the city.

Since the troops were supposed to be policing the city, there was no one to really prevent them from doing anything they wanted. Most people and animals kept their doors shut, their curtains drawn, and their mouths clamped. To be noticed meant certain trouble.

Of course, Maximilian knew all this. He was, technically, one of King Adax's elite soldiers, quite an accomplishment really for a coyote with no connections. So, as long as Anna kept the cape on, he explained, she would be safe from inquiry—most likely.

But it wasn't so simple.

They were walking through the streets deep in the bazaar, which, despite the late hour, was teeming with people. Soldiers who had been drinking and brawling seemed to be everywhere. A few animals were even shaving their own fur and selling it cheap. Anna felt more and more uncomfortable as they pressed on through the cacophony of the marketplace.

"How much further?" Anna asked.

"Not much, stay close," Maximilian instructed over his shoulder.

They were just reaching the edge of the bazaar, on the last street actually, when from under a shadowed awning a man called out, "Hey, Howl, who's the new recruit?" The man stepped into the dry nighttime street. A lamp from the opposite wall of the alley revealed he was missing an eye and most of his teeth.

Anna shuffled behind Maximilian shyly, feeling much more a little girl than a world traveller.

"New desert scout," Maximilian lied.

What's he talking about? Anna thought. She had a hard time deciphering lies.

The man grunted and stepped forward. He reached right over Maximilian and grabbed at Anna's chest. His grip caught cape, jacket, and the pendant that hung from her neck all in one fist. Anna was immobilized. He picked her up without effort and brought her enchanting face right up against his grotesque one.

"Do you know who I am?" His breath was loathsome.

Anna looked down pleadingly to Maximilian for help; his eyes were wide. "Put me down!" she demanded, turning back to the brute.

The man laughed and spittle came out of his mouth onto her red jacket, "I don't like your attitude, *Scout*."

"I'm no Scout, I'm a *Captain*, and I'm ordering you to put me down." Anna was dead serious.

The near-toothless ruffian's arms shook with mocking laughter. As her body shuddered in his grip, he caught a glimpse of the pendant underneath her layers. The ruby sparkled in the lamplight, drawing the brute's attention. He licked his fat lips and brought up his other hand to rip apart her clothes. Almost too easily, he tore the cloth and popped the top button off the girl's jacket, with another motion he ripped the precious necklace from her.

"No!" she protested, "Give it back!" She flailed in his arms, kicking his torso.

"A lot of spunk in this girl, Howl." The hideous man laughed again.

"Let her go, Colonel, she'll behave," Maximilian offered timidly.

"I will not behave!" Anna retaliated in her little voice, not understanding Maximilian's plea or their very apparent helplessness. She continued to struggle against his grip and to reach for her pendant ferociously.

Maximilian was beginning to see that Anna was incapable of letting an injustice go on for too long, and he could also see in her eyes that she was slowly changing from scared girl into dangerous captain.

She was reaching for her pistol!

"Colonel," Maximilian was talking as fast as he could, "she is a…jokester. She's kidding you. We were just on our way, in fact, at this very moment, even at such a late hour, to report to King Adax himself that she's discovered something in the desert that I'd never seen myself, a…a…a new dune! Possibly developed over the last season of sandstorms. It's a quite complicated geological formation, you know, out there in the sand—"

Anna had just managed to get a grip on her pistol when the Colonel, who was growing bored anyway and wasn't interested in getting between even a made-up meeting of King Adax and anyone, set the girl down. "Alright, alright," he said begrudgingly, "I'll let you go."

"Give me back my pendant." Anna said.

"This?" he held up the girl's irreplaceable leather-strapped, ruby pendant.

"It's an important new insignia for scouts of the king and absolutely must be worn at the meeting. Give it back to her."

Anna couldn't tell if Maximilian was lying or helping or both.

The ugly colonel grunted and threw the pendant back at Anna. She snatched it deftly out of the air and tied it back around her neck. With an angered look, she flipped her ripped jacket lapels as best she could to cover the jewel again.

"Let's go," Maximilian tugged at her sleeve.

Anna was still enraged at being picked up. Little girl or not, she was still a captain. A great captain! But before her passion could build into an outburst she saw a few other soldiers in red capes approaching from behind the colonel. They looked like trouble. She swallowed her bravery and squinted hard at the group. With a defiant snort of air, she turned and followed Maximilian around the corner.

"Hurry," Maximilian said.

"Who was that?" Anna demanded.

"Part of the king's army."

"Wait, they're on our side?" Anna couldn't believe it.

"Yes. No. Sort of. Just come on!" Maximilian led Anna through a series of roads and underpasses and crawlspaces. Through alleys that got narrower and narrower with each turn, until finally they came to a small door tucked between two buildings.

An elaborate clockwork puzzle served as its lock. Maximilian shifted the pieces, and as they clicked together the door popped away from its frame. Pulling the door open, he stepped to the side and gestured for Anna to descend into the dark cellar that opened before them.

"After you," he said and closed the door.

CHAPTER 5

Anna was quiet as she stood patiently in the dark of the cellar. She heard Maximilian shuffling around, some pots clanging, some papers and things tumbling off their shelves and desktops.

Maximilian let out a slight howl as he stubbed his foot on the corner of a table. Finally, he found the lamp he was looking for. With a turn of a small key at its base, the room was set aglow by warm lamplight. Anna noticed how red it made his gray fur look.

The coyote looked up from the table and into her eyes, then quickly turned away embarrassed and pretending to search for something else.

As she took in her surroundings, she decided that she liked the place. It was cozy and small, and it was clearly built specifically for Maximilian—all of the fixtures and furniture were his size. Amazingly, they were just right for her as well. It felt homey.

She sighed contentedly. "You live here?" she asked, taking off her red jacket and slinging it on the couch.

"Yes. Sometimes. This is my old residence. Before I was in service of the king."

"It's nice." She plopped down at the table.

Maximilian didn't respond.

"What a night!" she exclaimed, her disposition returning to her. "But, hey, I thought we were going to the palace?"

"We most certainly will, but it's so late, I thought it best to wait until the morning." Maximilian couldn't believe how many lies he was telling Anna. Even after she saved his life, he was still lying to her. He hated it. She had more heart that Maximilian ever would, and he liked her for it. She was fierce, that wasn't in question after the fight with Larraby and the encounter in the bazaar. But she was also innocent. She possessed a spirit and strength of character that made her unquestionably good. Maximilian knew it in his gut.

"Okay," Anna said, without questioning it. She yawned and got up from the table to lie down on the couch by her jacket. "So, what happened with that big, ugly guy in the market? Why'd he stop us?"

"Oh, him, he's just a…a *grouch*." But it wasn't true. The truth was that Maximilian was not part of the same volunteer army that the one-eyed Colonel was. Yes, Maximilian was a scout, but he was a slave as well. It infuriated him to even think about it. King Adax had control over everyone—that was the truth. It was the one fact that haunted him every night. It was why he had to bring Anna back to the king. Why he had to turn her in, her and her flying ship.

It was the reason he had to betray her.

Maximilian wanted to confess, wanted to tell Anna everything. In fact, he wanted to help her. But he couldn't, he just couldn't...if only he could stop lying to her.

"A grouch, huh? He almost took my pendant."

"Lucky he didn't keep it." Maximilian said, still melancholy in his thoughts.

"I would've got it back," Anna said slyly.

"Why is it so important anyway?"

"Well, a long time ago, there was a city in the jungle—"

"The jungle?" Maximilian was suddenly alert. It was a rare thing to hear any stories of the jungle, especially ones that might be true. He had to know more.

"Yep, the jungle. And the city was perfect. There were wells of fresh water and singing and flowers everywhere! And everyone should've been happy because of the king. He was a really good king." Anna looked down, saddened. "But they weren't. There was an evil jaguar who called himself Deces. He was always jealous of the king and so one day, he snuck into the palace and broke into the king's chambers."

Both Anna and Maximilian were on the edge of their seats as she told the story with great enthusiasm. "Deces tried to steal the crown, but he couldn't do it. The crown was too heavy!" She laughed. "It must've weighed, like, a million pounds! The king is so strong he's the only one who can pick it up, you see?"

"Yes, so the king punished the jaguar?"

"No. Deces should've been punished, he deserved it, but the king showed mercy on him instead. Then he pulled one of the jewels out of the crown and gave it to Deces, and told him that with it, he had the power to do *anything*."

"The power to do anything?" Maximilian asked confused.

"Well, anything *good*. And—"

"Wait! The jewel from the crown is—that's your pendant!" Maximilian exclaimed, guessing the obvious. Then realizing he was far too excited by the young girl's story, seemed to almost blush, well, as much as a coyote ever could blush.

"Exactly!" Anna said, matching his excitement. "That ruby from the crown is this ruby," she held up the pendant. "And when Deces had it, he ran away—*far* away. But even with the ruby from the king's crown right around his neck, Deces still didn't want to do anything good. So, the king sent me to go and get it back, because I'm the best pilot he's got!"

"And how'd you get it back?"

"I killed Deces." She crossed her arms.

"You killed the jaguar?"

"Sure did. I thought he had me for a while. He stabbed me, actually, but I stabbed him too. He stayed down, and I got up. And that's that."

Maximilian leaned back against the chair and breathed, "It's quite the story, Captain." Maximilian looked contemplative, skeptical perhaps.

"Don't you believe me?"

Maximilian thought for a moment then decided. "Yes, I think I do."

"Good! I'm glad to hear it, Max. Cause it's true, I would never lie to you." Anna yawned again and slumped back into the cushions with a stretch. "I'm sleepy!" The precocious girl nestled in against the cushions and sighed, "Good night, Max."

"Good night, Captain." Maximilian said, and his guilt seemed to punch him in the gut.

***

In a desert as vast and hot and oppressive as Highsand Desert, one of the greatest miracles is an oasis. The Edges' base was located, of course, in the desert. Lieutenant Larraby always liked to think that it was his leadership that made it all possible, but in reality, it was because the base was located around an oasis. It was the small pool buried deep underground in a cave that was the central component of the Edges' resistance to King Adax.

The Pool, as it was called for simplicity's sake, was big enough to support the small group of people that lived at the base—mainly the leadership of the resistance and its few "soldiers." Every other member of the Edges had to hide their true allegiance and live covertly in Dung Dune City or its surrounding villages, which were all under the rule of King Adax.

But what was most important at this moment to Apple, as he approached the base, was none of that, but rather the fact that to get to the Edges' base, he would have to use a ladder. His foot, now with one less toe, was in the worst pain he'd ever experienced. And although it was rather sickening to imagine, Apple couldn't help but picture his boot totally filled with blood. He gagged at the squishing sound coming from his boot.

Tonight is no night for wimpy behavior, Apple thought. "Larraby is counting on me!" He said aloud to give himself the determination he would need. He set his face with a look of equal determination and headed down the ladder ouch-ing and wincing with each rung. "Oo, ah, eee, ah, oo, ah!"

When he reached the bottom of the ladder, after having made plenty of commotion and noise, there was already a small crowd gathered. Apple spoke quickly to all of them not concerned about any permissions or clearances that his information should have been processed through—the Edges were normally much more organized. But this, an airship, was unprecedented. There was no protocol for an event of this magnitude.

He was still huffing from coming down the ladder when he started to say, "Something wonderful has happened!" but then a quick jolt of pain shot through his whole body. He grimaced as he bent over to grab his foot, "My toe's been shot off!"

"And that's wonderful?" someone from the back of the crowd asked.

"No, no, no, that's not wonderful, that's horrible!" he grunted through the pain. "An airship has crashed in the desert!"

The room erupted into questions on all sides of him.

"Airship!?!"

"Where?"

"Whose ship is it?"

"Where'd it come from!?"

Apple did his best to shout over everyone, "I don't know, I don't know, but Lieutenant Larraby and Truck are at the base of Bertha and have called for help—immediately!"

The crowd split in a hundred directions. People scrambled over one another in a frenzy to pick up homemade weapons of all varieties and put on their goggles and jackets. And rightly they did to scramble. A flying ship meant trouble and, possibly, an outsider—someone who had broken King Adax's no-flying rules. But it also meant hope, because they suddenly weren't alone, and everyone knew it.

Within a few minutes the cave had completely emptied, leaving Apple alone to take off his boot and inspect his severed toe.

By the time the group of rag-tag Edges had arrived at Bertha, Larraby and Truck had barely begun to uncover the Sky-Lion. They were beginning to lose hope. But when the lieutenant saw the Edges come over the dune, his spirit returned. He organized them into teams to dig out the rest of the airship. The sun was already up. They didn't have much time before it would be far too hot to dig. They had to move fast to transport the airship.

For all the questions in his mind, and in the minds of all the Edges, that was the one thing Larraby was sure of. They had to move the vessel and hide it from the king.

If Burp and Belch returned, or worse if King Adax came himself, he would have in his possession the most powerful piece of machinery in all of Highsand. Because this machine, if it really was an airship, gave the power to fly, the ability to leave the desert.

It was obvious—control of the airship was crucial. Larraby would never be able to forgive himself if he allowed the ship to fall into the hands of the king. The Edges had to hide it, and hide it well. Their work was spurred by the danger.

Through the efforts of the entire base camp of Edges, the ship was excavated in less than an hour. But once unearthed and examined, Larraby realized it would be far too small to hold everyone for an escape from the desert. And maybe more importantly, it was much too heavily damaged to fly in its current state.

Even having never seen an airship, he knew that.

So did the Edges. Their hope and excitement was undone, as utterly broken as the Sky-Lion itself. Larraby could see it.

They needed inspiration.

He pulled his hat from under his belt and donned it with a flourish; its wide brim, though slashed from his fight with Captain Anna, gave him an impressive air that he needed now.

"Good persons of the Edges!" He started climbing aboard the wrecked deck of the Sky-Lion, forcing himself up even with the difficulty of his mechanical leg. "I know your fears—that this airship will not be enough to save us." His yellow beard glistened in the waxing morning light. "You fear that our waiting and hoping has been in vain. But I tell you, I have seen the captain of this ship, and they are brave and strong."

Larraby didn't want to mention this "captain" was also a *little girl*. Lucky for him, as they exchanged glances, he knew Truck wasn't going to say anything about her either—she was strong and brave after all.

"I don't know if the captain of this vessel will help us, but if we've fought for anything good, then it's this moment. All of the years of fighting come down to this day. Whatever happens with this technology will change everything for us, for our families. If we can get this ship flying, we may finally find a way out of Highsand. But *we* must have the ship. If that *beetle* gets it," people and animals in the crowd spit on the ground, "he'll destroy it, or use it against us. Either way, its destruction or application by the king will crush our chance at freedom. Everything is at stake now. It's not just this machine. It's all the power that comes with it, all the advancements it would bring. We must hide this ship!"

Everyone was quiet, weighing their thoughts, thinking about how long they'd waited for a moment like this. Suddenly, the Edges seemed to surge back with renewed life at Lieutenant Larraby's words. They began pushing and dragging the Sky-Lion deeper into the desert.

CHAPTeR 6

Anna awoke to the smell of food cooking and, rolling over on the couch, smiled that she had not imagined it. She had totally forgotten about eating in all of the excitement of last night's adventure and didn't realize how hungry she'd become. Whatever Maximilian was cooking, the smell of it had her practically drooling.

She perked up on the couch and stretched, pulling her knees up to her chest and proving that her high energy started the moment she opened her eyes. "Got enough over there for me too?"

"Of course, Captain Tomahawk," Maximilian replied with a genuine smile. "You like beans and vegetables?"

"Eeew, no!" Anna said. But when she moved over to the pot of simmering food, she realized resistance to the savory aroma would be futile. "But I guess I'll try some."

"It's my special recipe, passed down from my grandfather and his father." Maximilian pulled a bowl from a stack of dishes on the counter and ladled a generous helping into it. "Eat up. You'll need your strength today."

"Are we going to see King Adax? About the Sky-Lion?" Anna asked interested.

"I…no, not yet."

"But I really need to get her fixed! The Sky-Lion being all injured like that," she sighed dramatically, throwing her arms out the sides. "It makes me terribly sad, Max."

Maximilian's face tightened at being called *Max* again. "It doesn't have feelings, Captain. It's inanimate. Can't be injured."

"If you'd been through as much as I have on the Sky-Lion, you'd think she's alive too," Anna said ominously, trying to spook the coyote. Then she dropped an elbow onto the table without manners and plopped her tilted head into her palm with a goofy smile, staring at the food. "Here goes nothing." She took a large spoonful of Maximilian's special dish.

"Well?"

"It's good!" Anna said with her mouth full. She started swinging her feet and eating hungrily.

"Good." Maximilian said, joining her at the table. "And perhaps I would think the same thing if I'd been along for a flying adventure. We'll get it fixed, and we will see King Adax soon enough. Believe me."

"Okay. I trust you, Max."

He took an uncomfortable bite. "Tell me something, how did you become the pilot of an airship? Why you, such a *young* girl?"

"Who says I'm young?"

Maximilian looked her over and shrugged.

Anna shrugged back, "I'm older than I look."

"Hmm," Maximilian grunted. "But how did you become a pilot?"

"I guess I just had to do it. It's why I was born, to be the best captain there ever was."

"You know other captains of other airships?"

"Nope," Anna said, clearing some of the meal off her chin with the back of her hand. She flashed him a wide smile of white teeth, "I'm the only one."

"That seems to make you very important, doesn't it?"

Anna stopped eating and set down her spoon, "Yeah. I suppose I am." Maximilian and Anna looked at each other before she began again, "But I thought you said King Adax could help fix the Sky-Lion. Isn't *he* a pilot?"

Maximilian couldn't help but chuckle in his coyote way. "The king a pilot? No, certainly not. Not yet, anyway." Maximilian got up to clear away Anna's dish as if to change the subject.

"So, if he's not a pilot, then how's he going to help fix her? The Sky-Lion is a very special airship, she's the best."

"I don't know, Captain. That's why we must speak with him."

"But not today?"

"No, tomorrow." Maximilian ran a paw across the top of his head, scratching a spot between his upright ears. "Today, I go talk to him alone."

"What do I do? Can't I come with?"

"You can stay here, and I expect you to. I don't need you wandering around in the streets getting kidnapped by anyone."

"Kidnapped? Max, I'm much too crafty of a coyote to be kidnapped," she said, poking fun.

"Even the best coyote can be caught up in things, Captain. So stay here."

"Well, I'm not promising anything. Sometimes I need an adventure."

"Please, Anna, for today—stay here." Maximilian was already buckling his belt with his new sword, getting ready to leave.

Anna just smiled mischievously.

Maximilian strapped on his goggles and walked out, locking the door behind him with its clockwork combination.

"Bye, Max!" Anna called through the door, but he didn't respond.

She slumped back into the chair and put her feet up on the table, rocking the chair on two legs. Now, in the daylight from the back windows, she had a chance to really look at the dwelling. Maximilian's home was rather remarkably unremarkable. Nothing of interest really stood out at all. The corners were corners. The walls were walls. There was a fireplace and the red couch and the table and chairs and lots of dishes. So many dishes, in fact, that it was a wonder Maximilian wasn't five times as large as he was. That many dishes only begged to be used. There were no books. The ink well on his small desk was empty, even though there was plenty of paper, and there was resoundingly nothing to look at and nothing to do.

Anna knew it would be a long, boring day waiting for Maximilian to return. She let out a hopeless groan and then finally spotted something interesting. A spider. It was high in the corner behind her. She slammed her chair down on all four legs and raced up to get a closer look.

"Hey!" she said to the spider, her voice as warm and friendly as she could make it, which was quite warm and quite friendly indeed.

The large spider craned its head toward her. The light from the window on the opposite side was beaming against the corner of the room where the spider sat. As Anna moved closer, her shadow was thrown upon the wall, and noticing it, she started playing with it. Pumping her arms like a strong man and giving herself antlers and then wings with the shadow.

Then, remembering the spider, she stopped with the shadow play. She was about to look back up to the little creature, when the shadow continued moving. It grew larger and broader than it should have, and then she recognized the silhouette, recognized the wide-brimmed hat and the big face, a face with a beard—a yellow beard. She knew at once—the man from the desert.

The window behind her shattered!

***

Maximilian was far away from his hidden apartment. Even with his excellent canine hearing, he didn't hear the window break, didn't hear the young Captain Anna Tomahawk scream in fright. His jaw was set, his head was high, and his cape was blowing behind him in the wind as he raced towards the palace of the king.

Maximilian didn't know in the least what he was going to say to King Adax. *I found a girl*, he thought sounded too mundane. *I found an airship*, seemed too incomplete. *I found an airship and the pilot is a small girl with a gun and sword*, sounded too unbelievable. He contemplated the things that he could say and couldn't believe that he was still confounded with it by the time he was bounding up the steps to the main gate of the palace.

Better to say less, he thought, *just in case and for her safety.*

The halls of the palace were filled with statues of scorpions and beetles. Not all the various, wonderful beetles the world over, but dung beetles. All of them were posed in the same pose. Whichever artist had sculpted them, Maximilian had always thought, must be absolutely without any sense of creativity. They were repulsive and miserable to look at, a true tribute to the king.

The throne room doors were already wide open as Maximilian reached the end of the hall. Inside was a collection of his least favorite persons—Burp and Belch, Sheena, and King Adax. King Adax sat on his throne with a contemptible look.

"I hope," the giant dung beetle started, "that you have some good news for me, Howl."

Maximilian bowed as was customary in the throne room. Without looking up, "Your Majesty, I have found an airship."

"Of course you did, you fool. What on it? These two idiots inform me that they buried it late last night. What took you so long?"

"They didn't bring it back?" Maximilian prodded, hoping that he didn't give away the hope in his voice.

"We tried to, Your Majesty," Burp said quickly.

"It was too big!" Belch said.

"I heard your story!" King Adax yelled at them. Turning back to the coyote, "You found *nothing*, Maximilian?"

Maximilian hesitated, not sure how to answer. He was afraid to tell King Adax about Anna. Afraid of what the king might do in his rage both to him and his young captain friend.

"I'm sorry, Your Majesty," was all Maximilian offered.

"Agh!" King Adax roared back, slamming his hard exoskeletal fists into his throne. "You're worthless!" He stood up and launched himself at the coyote, picking him up by the throat with two of his arms. "Give me one reason I shouldn't crush you right now!?"

Maximilian couldn't breathe, let alone give a response if he would have even known what to say. Something, even with the grip of death around his neck, was stopping him from betraying Anna.

"Your Majesty," Sheena interrupted, trying to calm him before he murdered the useful scout. "Perhaps it was an unmanned craft?"

The king slowly lessened his grip around Maximilian's throat and dropped him. Maximilian shook like his instincts told him, correcting his messed neck-fur.

"What?" The king demanded.

Sheena's wrinkles turned extra pale as she answered the angry beetle, "Perhaps, there was no crew aboard the ship. That would leave nothing to find but the wreckage, like the hedgehogs reported, Your Majesty."

King Adax doubted that very much. In fact, he hoped that Sheena was wrong because he knew he couldn't build or rebuild an airship unless he acquired knowledge from some genuine flyers. Still, he seemed to calm a bit as he considered it. But a little calm from King Adax was still a thunderstorm of anger. He was most unpredictable when angered.

"Listen to me very carefully, I don't care if it takes you the rest of your pathetic lives," he pointed to Maximilian, Burp, and Belch each with a separate arm, "the three of you will bring me that ship. Drag it here if you have to. Bring it through the main gate if you must, but get me that airship!" King Adax fumed, his beak-like mouth snarled back in fury.

"Your Majesty," Maximilian, Burp and Belch said in unison. They bowed and hurried out of the room.

CHAPTER 7

Anna had given up her pleas of "Where are you taking me?!" and demands of "Let me go!" hours ago. She was inside a thick woven basket, barely able to see through its sides. But she knew she was back in the desert.

The young and feisty captain had put up a courageous fight in Maximilian's home. But having left her sword and pistol on the couch cushions, she had naught but her little fists to combat her kidnapper. Fists proved no match for Lieutenant Larraby.

How it all happened was quite simple. Larraby, knowing that the airship without a captain would be worthless, put together a scheme to enter Dung Dune City and find the girl pilot. He would spirit her away before the evil beetle ever saw her.

Larraby had been lucky, and he knew it. Many members of the Edges lived in Dung Dune City. They all hated the king and risked much to live there, and though they had no strength to openly oppose King Adax and his army, they were brave enough to work as spies for the rebellion. It was these very spies who had informed Larraby that the girl was being hidden in Maximilian Howl's home.

Maximilian, for reasons Larraby couldn't guess, had decided *not* to take the girl directly to the king. And the Edges, although their base was far from Dung Dune City, had managed to convey the message back to their leader. It was an opportunity that only a fool would have passed up, and Larraby was anything but a fool.

He knew he might not have another chance, so he set out immediately with a small team of his best men—with the exception of Apple who was still grieving his lost toe—to subdue the girl in Maximilian's home, to capture her and bring her back to the Edges base. Undeniably, the Edges on the whole had been lucky further still, when Maximilian abandoned the young firecracker to loneliness. Once they knew she was by herself, it had been almost easy. Without her weapons she was hardly a match for the striking lieutenant.

Now, she was theirs. She was their captive and their hope. She was their key, the key to escape the figurative dungeon of King Adax's desert empire. If of course, she would cooperate.

They reached the base and lowered the basket, containing the still kicking captain, down to the floor. Anna noticed the change in temperature and the lack of sand being spat through the basket's frame as she was dragged along. Of course, the gravity difference and the swinging of the basket were also giveaways to the fact that she was descending.

Captured and being buried alive? She wondered.

Highsand Desert was turning out to be a rather unwelcoming place to the greatest adventurer in the world. She missed Maximilian. But still she wasn't afraid. She was brave.

The basket hit the ground hard and Anna knocked her head against the lid. She let out a quick, "Ouch." Larraby untied the top and lifted off the lid. She popped up immediately like a jack-in-the-box.

The crowd, sans any other little girls, gaped at her and began whispering amongst themselves.

The yellow-bearded man looked at them over his shoulder slightly annoyed. "I am Lieutenant Larraby. I am the *humble* leader of these people," he gestured to the crowd. "Who are you? Why have you come?"

Anna looked around confused and skeptical, but she *never-never, ever-ever* missed a chance to tell anyone who she was.

"I'm Captain Anna Tomahawk of the Sky-Lion, and I'm the meanest-dueling, quickest-shooting *pilot* there ever was. I can shoot a match head off the stick from a mile away with my eyes closed. And I'm giving you one chance, right now, to surrender!"

Her memorized and carefully rehearsed claim-to-fame seemed to fall slightly, but only slightly, lightweight on the ears of her captors. She attributed her lack of impression to the lack of her rapier and pistol. She had barely noticed that she had struck a mighty pose—with her hands on her hips and her chest out—still standing in the basket.

Larraby, impressed but trying not to seem it, wiped his mustache and crossed his arms. "We won't be surrendering, Captain Tomahawk. Why are you here?"

Anna shrugged with her shoulders and hands. "I don't know, you brought me here."

Larraby and the crowd nearly fell over dumbfounded.

Recovering, the lieutenant cleared his throat, "You're the pilot of an airship, aren't you? And you came to Highsand Desert. What is your purpose?"

"Oh, that part. I got shot down," Anna said honestly. "I was on my way home to the jungle."

The crowd gushed with whispers at her nonchalant mention of the jungle.

"Explain," Larraby ordered.

"Well, I was on a mission across the world to get this," without taking it off she held up her ruby pendant, the crowd awed. "And, of course, 'cause I'm the greatest," she smiled, "I got it." She stuffed the pendant back under her shirt. "Then on my way back I got stranded on an island for a while, because of a storm. It's kind of a long story, but anyway, I figured crossing this desert was the most di-rect route home."

Larraby didn't know what was more shocking: her words or how weirdly personable she was for being a recent victim of a kidnapping. She certainly didn't seem like one of King Adax's servants. She was too open, too willing to share. He stepped close to the basket. "How do we know any of what you say is true?"

Anna shrugged. "I could take you there after we fix the Sky-Lion."

"I'm sure you could." Larraby stared at her and huffed. "I'd appreciate some evidence for a story so steamin' hard to believe."

"I'm not a liar," Anna said.

"How do you know Howl?"

"Howl?"

"Yes, Maximilian Howl, the scout. You were with him."

"Oh! You mean Max. He's my friend."

"Your friend?" Larraby asked, as the crowd quieted to try to hear their conversation.

"Yep. He made me breakfast." Her smile leveled out as her tone changed, "Why were you trying to hurt him?" Her accusatory look pushed Lieutenant Larraby back.

"He's a steamin' traitor."

"He is not!" Anna declared loudly to the room, her voice pushing Larraby further away from her and the basket. She climbed out to stand on the ground. "He's my friend and he's nice."

"He's a traitor, girl." Larraby spoke with conviction and force. "He betrayed the location of the Edges' camp years ago and brought about the death of many innocent lives."

Anna couldn't help but wonder about his accusation. She hadn't known Maximilian very long. Still, she had always been a good judge of character. If it was true, it didn't matter, because Anna was loyal to her friends. She grunted and decided to believe the best about her coyote companion no matter what Larraby said, even if that meant forgiving a traitor.

"Well, he's different now."

"That doesn't matter." Larraby said quickly.

"Yes, it does!"

"No, it doesn't."

"Yes, it does!"

"No, it doesn't!" Larraby overturned the basket behind her in frustration.

"Yes. It. Does." Anna said through her teeth for the final time, stepping closer to the lieutenant.

Larraby wiped his mouth and pulled on his beard as he and Anna fell into a stare-off. But then, something like magic happened, and Larraby could have never expected it. It wasn't that he couldn't hold her gaze. He was used to staring through clouds of desert sand in the hot sun without blinking, a staring contest would be simple. It was something else. As the lieutenant looked into her young determined face, he softened. Her eyes were pure and bright. Coupled with her attempt to look intimidating, they made him want to laugh, as if both innocence and courage were dancing together.

They made him happy, happier than he had been in a long time. After a few moments, he had completely lost his train of thought. He had been hypnotized. And though Larraby didn't want to admit it, he could feel in his heart that Anna was something special.

Anna was still thinking about the possibility that Maximilian might be a traitor.

While they were both lost in thought, Anna's little face and Larraby's bright yellow beard had inched closer and closer to one another, until her nose almost touched his.

"*What are* the Edges?" Anna finally asked, startling Larraby and cutting off his trance.

Larraby shook his head to clear it; dust fell out of his beard. He stepped back abruptly, "Not what, *who* are the Edges? We are." He gestured with his head back towards the group, "We are the force against the slavery and imprisonment of King Adax's evil empire." The crowd spit on the floor of the cavern, everyone wanted to spit at the mention of King Adax's name so it took a moment.

"King Adax?" Anna's face twisted in bewilderment. "He's going to help fix the Sky-Lion."

"King Adax—fix your airship?" Larraby quizzed.

"Yep. That's what Max said."

"Impossible, the king would never."

Anna didn't say anything; it was hard to tell who was lying. Maximilian or Larraby?

"Maximilian is a traitor, Anna." Larraby continued, "He has deceived you. And he will hand you over to the king, like he handed us over to the king. Once a traitor, always a traitor."

"No," Anna said confidently. "You're wrong, he's different now."

"You're a foolish girl." Larraby adjusted his hat, "How is he different? What changed him?"

"Not what, *who*." Anna stood with a hint of a smile on her face. She was calm and sure without any judgment.

"You?"

"Yep, me."

"Because you're not from Highsand, right? You're *special*," Larraby said with sarcasm.

Anna just looked at him with her shimmering, pure eyes. She didn't need to answer.

In her silence, Larraby fished through his mind, trying to make sense of it. Could it really be? Could this young girl be telling the truth? Was she, in fact, everything she claimed to be?

Everything the Edges hoped she would be?

Larraby tried to look with his heart and not his eyes. She was a pilot. She could fly. And if what she was saying was really true, then she *did know* the way from the desert to the jungle. Knew the way to freedom.

But more important than any other quality she possessed, Larraby thought, she was good. They had hoped for all these things before. They had hoped for these things for years in their dreams of a rescuer. Even as they moved the Sky-Lion from Bertha to its new hiding place they held onto that hope. Now, seeing her in person and hearing her talk, that hope was finally being realized.

"You really are from the jungle," Larraby said in a wide-eyed whisper, understanding how close freedom now was.

"What?" said Anna, not hearing.

"You really are from the jungle," Larraby said again louder, loud enough that the crowd behind him could hear also.

"Yeah, I just told you that, weren't you listening?" she said with a stretch and slight exasperation in her voice.

Larraby's eyes welled with tears as he tried to blink them away and maintain his composure. "If you are who you say you are, then we need your help, Captain."

"So, am I not kidnapped anymore?"

"No, I'm sorry for that."

Anna stretched again, still trying to work out the stiffness from being stuffed into the basket. "It's okay, but don't do it again."

"Of course," Larraby paused, not knowing where to start. "I want you to help fight in our rebellion against the king."

"Oh," said Anna, "Well, I don't fight people just 'cause. I never even got a chance to meet King Adax, why would I fight him?"

"Because he's an oppressor."

"But Max said he was going to help fix the Sky-Lion."

"He won't. Maximilian lied. That steamin' dung beetle is evil. He would never help you. He has laws against flying."

"Hmm," Anna sounded, considering the words.

"I don't know what Maximilian is up to, but the king, I can promise you, Captain, is ruthless."

"Well Max isn't. He's my friend."

"If he's working for King Adax, he can't be good."

"Maybe he isn't working for King Adax, maybe you just *think* he is," Anna said, trying to persuade Larraby.

"I don't think that's possible. The king is hard to deceive; he's a master of lies himself."

"What do you mean?"

"It's a lot to explain. The king would tell you a very different story, but it'd all be a steamin' conspiracy. The truth is that before my time, before the Edges had ever dreamed of leaving Highsand, King Adax was just another creature in the desert. But he was too steamin' proud to stay that way. He wanted to control things. The story goes, that he started forming alliances, muscling out the people who wouldn't join him. Killing them. He took over the land, hoarded the resources, and eventually declared himself king."

"Why didn't anybody stop him?"

"He was too strong. He started systematically eliminating his opposition, ensuring his position of power. Then, somehow, as time passed, he grew bigger. Literally."

"How big can a dung beetle get?" Anna tilted her head to the side.

"Huge," Larraby said. "It's crazy to admit I've even thought it, but it's as if his size is linked to his control over Highsand. For years King Adax's supremacy continued to develop politically. And, of course, physically he thrived in the desert, all of it seeming to contribute to making him bigger and stronger. Now, all of Highsand fears him. He rules the desert with absolute authority. His word is law."

"What about you guys? If he doesn't like you, then—" Anna didn't want to finish the thought.

"Yes," Larraby said. "He tries to stop us by any means he can—murder, spies, ultimatums we can't ignore. He rations resources from suspected members, the only way we can fight is by staying hidden."

"So, he doesn't know about this place then huh?" Anna looked around at the stone walls. Copper-colored, metal supports framed every open hallway.

"No, it's a secret that must be kept. The location of our last hideout was compromised by your friend the coyote," Larraby leaned back against the wall.

"Well, he would never do that now."

"It would be the end of us if he did. In this cave sits the last oasis large enough to support our headquarters. It's not enough for a full-fledged rebellion, but it's enough to keep us trying. The biggest and deepest oasis-well in the entire desert is behind the highest walls and most secure forces in the center of Dung Dune City. The king's palace is right next to it."

"And he won't share at all?"

"He'll share as long as he can present himself as the guardian of the water, the provider for all the citizens' needs and protection. Half the steamin' fools believe him. The rest have accepted it as the way things are. They've given up." Larraby reached down to squeeze his mechanical knee in frustration.

"What happened to your leg?"

Larraby frowned, "It's a long story."

"Oh, well, I like it."

Larraby blushed. "I liked my old leg," he said, trying vainly to accept the awkward compliment.

"At least you still have something, even if you're not strong enough to fight King Adax. So, does everybody think he's a bad guy?"

"Most do, but people are afraid. The king is strong, and he grows stronger. He's still power-hungry. Evil. He forces the citizens into submission. Keeping precious resources to reward his army. All the while, the people around him suffer and starve."

"Maybe I can help talk to him, ya know, straighten things out."

"I'm glad to hear you say that," Larraby smiled and his yellow beard rose with his cheeks.

The silent crowd pressed closer with happy excitement.

"We've waited so long for this moment, waited for help. Waited for *something* to tip the scale in our favor."

"*Someone*, you mean," Anna said.

"Yes."

The Edges all stared at the girl with eager faces.

She understood their misery, and because she did, she had the potential to be the rescuer strong enough to help them out of it.

"Well, I don't care how big this beetle is, if that's his attitude, I don't like it. And I think it's about time he picked on somebody his own size. Me."

Larraby shook his head as he tried to adjust to the girl's precocious attitude. "Captain, I think you might be exactly what we've been waiting for."

CHAPTER 8

Meanwhile, Burp and Belch and Maximilian were riding headlong into the desert on the back of the Worm. They were headed directly towards the great dune Bertha and the crash site where the buried airship awaited, the airship that Maximilian knew to be Captain Anna's Sky-Lion.

Unbeknownst to any of them, it was, of course, already long gone. Larraby and the Edges had successfully moved it. But the three didn't know that yet. Maximilian was too busy regretting his canine sense of hearing as he found it impossible to block out the sound of Burp and Belch arguing.

Still, his thoughts were far away, back in Dung Dune City, where Anna sat in his home. Probably bored, he imagined, an adventuring world-traveller like Anna locked in a tiny cellar apartment. He had not been able to go back to the apartment, obviously, not with Burp and Belch following him around. And he couldn't very well refuse the order to bring the airship back to King Adax as soon as possible. Though, he was wondering what would happen if he didn't bring it back. Maximilian certainly didn't *want* to bring the ship to King Adax now.

Maximilian, like many others, frequently forgot exactly how powerful the dung beetle was. And like many evils, when not experienced for a while, one tends to think of them as less powerful and controlling than they are. But, assuredly, King Adax was quite strong. After Maximilian's recent exposure just hours ago, he knew again and keenly, that King Adax would never help Anna fix her airship. He shuddered to think at all what the evil king would do to his friend, the precious Captain Tomahawk.

He had to think quickly. He couldn't let Burp and Belch find that airship again. He needed a plan. His resources were extremely limited. He had his sword, but he wasn't about to fight the two hedgehogs. It was too dangerous and too bloody, and for whatever reason, he imagined they might not deserve to be killed. Something in his heart told him that Anna might not want them dead. The coyote kept thinking about how she had spared Lieutenant Larraby and his comrades. How she didn't want to fight him, when they first met either. For whatever reason, mercy seemed more important after being around Captain Tomahawk.

He couldn't stop thinking about her. "I have to protect her. I have to do something," the coyote said to himself.

He gave a quick bark and straightened his belt before he sauntered up the neck of the Worm towards where the two hedgehogs sat bickering. "Where are you fools going?"

Burp and Belch simultaneously grabbed the brakes on either side of their chairs and slammed them forward. The Worm came to a grinding halt, spilling Maximilian forward in a tumble between their seats. They both leaned over and looked down at him.

"What do you mean—" Burp started.

"Where are we going?" Belch finished.

Maximilian straightened his goggles around his coyote ears. "This is not the correct way."

"Yes it is. It's buried at Bertha, just beyond that dune there."

"Bertha!" Maximilian laughed, acting, "Why you wouldn't know a cliff-dune from a molehill." Burp and Belch looked at each other confused.

"Yes, we would." Belch said.

"Yeah, sure we would!" Burp said, "Wouldn't we, Belch?"

"Yeah…wouldn't we?"

"Yeah…I think." Burp answered again.

"Well, it's a good thing I'm here," Maximilian chimed in, waving away their back-and-forth. "The ship crashed that direction," he said, pointing back towards the tail of the Worm.

The hedgehogs turned together to look the direction he pointed, and then looked back down at the coyote.

Maximilian didn't move.

"That's the opposite direction," said Belch.

"Yeah. Are you *sure*, Howl?"

"Of course I'm sure. But if you insist on going this direction, I'll simply have to inform King Adax that it took us twice as long to bring him the airship because *you* couldn't remember where you buried it." Maximilian licked his teeth.

Both of the hedgehogs spiked up and spun the Worm around. Maximilian stood between them and turned forward again. He put a paw on the backs of each of their chairs and let out a sigh as the Worm clanged and grinded across the desert. He had bought some time, but time for what?

He had no idea.

His next immediate concern would be to get the two argumentative engineers to turn the Worm around after a few hours without them noticing he was simply taking the long, long way to Bertha.

Then an idea came to him. A simple idea but, he thought, a rather clever one. He would sleep. A short nap was all he really needed. Then when Burp and Belch woke him up, he would be able to deny having any part of getting them lost. He climbed back towards the middle of the Worm's metallic body, found a flat hump there, and with a swirl of his cape and a slip of his goggles over his eyes, he settled down for his ingenious nap.

***

Larraby and Captain Tomahawk had walked together for what felt like a half-dozen miles before coming to a rocky cliff-face in the desert. It wasn't very high on its own, but the sand-blown dune on top stretched its height to nearly a hundred feet. In the center of the cliff-face was a cave.

When they got close Larraby pulled a metal tool out of his pack and with a couple twists and a few cranks, a thin metal coil at the top started to glow bright orange, illuminating the inside of the cave as they entered. He held it up like a torch to spread the light out. The cave's path led down steeply.

"I like your wand."

"Thank you, we Edges invented it. We call it a *radio*."

"A radio?" Anna smiled. "That's a strange name for it."

"I don't see how. We're all inventors. Only thing we can't seem to figure out is how to fly. Flight capability would give us one of the most important experiences. Something we can't invent. Freedom."

The young girl seemed not to notice his philosophical musings.

"The Sky-Lion!" Captain Anna beamed when they emerged into the cave's main chamber. The airship sat like a great dragon in its lonely home. She snatched the radio from Lieutenant Larraby's hand and began cranking it as she slid down a series of rocks toward the bottom of the chamber. Whooping in delight as she slid.

"Yes, Anna," Larraby shouted down after her as he made his slow descent. "We salvaged *it* from the desert."

"*Her* not it." Anna craned her head to either side, "And what did you do to her? Looks more broken than when I crashed!"

"Ahem, well, you see—"

"...and call me Captain Anna." She finished with a wink over her shoulder.

"*Captain* Anna," Larraby said with exaggeration as he climbed down the last few rocks. He twisted the valve on his knee, and the gage spun around as the pressure was released from his leg, "the ship—"

"Sky-Lion," she corrected.

"The *Sky-Lion*," Larraby started again with mild irritation, retightening the wingnut, "was already heavily damaged, as you know. Unfortunately, we had to break the vessel more in order to drag her in here."

"You dragged her too!"

"Stop objecting to everything! We had to!" Larraby said, discombobulated and flailing his arms. Regaining his composure and fixing his hat he started again with a deep breath, "Now, that it's safe we can fix it. Then you show us how to steamin' get out of Highsand."

"Out of Highsand? Just keep going that way," she pointed in two directions spun a circle and laughed. "It's really easy to find the edge. You just have to trust it's there, and keep going till you get to it."

"We've tried, believe me. I've tried myself many times. It's farther than you think."

"It's closer than you know."

"You like to disagree with me, girl, don't you?"

"When you're right, you're right. And I'm right." She smiled again and spun again towards the Sky-Lion, her ponytail swishing behind her head. "We gotta get her out of the cave."

"Not possible. We have no where to hide the vessel."

"Well, we can't fix her in here, Lieutenant Larraby sir. Once she's back to her full size with the wings spread out and the dorsal fin straightened out and the bag inflated, well, ya know, out, she's not going to fit through the entrance!"

Lieutenant Larraby thought about it for a moment. "Hmm. You're right. We'll have to repair her in the open, under heavy guard, of course. Do you think you can fix it?"

"Of course I can. I'm the best. Nobody knows how to fix the Sky-Lion better than me." Captain Tomahawk threw back her shoulders with pride.

"You just tell me what you need, and the Edges will help you get it. The radio." Larraby held out his hand.

"Oh, sorry! Here!" and she tossed it back to him.

Larraby juggled it, desperately trying not to drop and break it.

"We have to find Max."

"It's a waste of time. He's no good, that coyote," Larraby discouraged.

"He can be if I say so."

"Anna, you—"

"Captain—" she corrected again.

"Captain, you have to trust me. He's with the king."

Captain Anna shook her head. "He's with me. He's my friend, and we have to find him. I won't fix the Sky-Lion without him. I promised I'd take him to see some leaves."

Lieutenant Larraby sighed and pulled on his yellow beard. He gnawed on the corner of his mustache and with reluctance let her win, for now. "Fine. We'll find Howl, we'll fix the Sky-Lion, and you'll show us the way out of Highsand."

"I'd love to," she smiled.

***

Much closer than Lieutenant Larraby and Captain Anna knew, King Adax's two top engineers rumbled by in the noisy, powerful Worm. Little did they know as they passed the cliff-face that they were going *by* the Sky-Lion not *to* the Sky-Lion.

"Stop!" Belch yelled.

Burp grabbed a hold of his brake and pulled back hard. The worm slowed and rested amidst a big cloud of dust and sand. He pushed one lens of his goggles up onto his brow and looked to his teammate. "I told you to pee before we left, Belch!"

"It's not that!" Belch sniffed the air. "We're going the wrong way. I'm positive we buried it that way." And he jerked a furry thumb back over his shoulder.

"Then, Maximilian lied to us?"

"He tricked us!" Belch agreed.

"That rotten, no good coyote. Why I'll stick all my quills in him!" Burp stood and started up the body on the top of the Worm, towards where Maximilian slept.

Belch opened a hatch on the side and pulled out a bob-ended, wire net. They walked towards Maximilian together.

Maximilian Howl had meant to only feign his sleep. But with all of his worrying about Anna and the adventure of the night before, he was exhausted. The call of the nap proved more powerful than the call of his wild instincts.

"Gotcha!" Burp and Belch yelled in unison as Maximilian awoke to find himself trapped under the net.

"What are you doing!? Let me out!"

"You lied to us," said Burp.

"Tricked us," said Belch.

"What are you talking about?" Maximilian said, expertly playing innocent. "Let me out of this net immediately."

"I don't think so, Maximilian. You deliberately told us the wrong direction—why?" Burp asked, breaking off one of his own quills to use as a spear. He poked Maximilian through the wire. It cut deeply into his arm, which started bleeding right away, turning his gray fur dark red.

Maximilian grunted and clutched at his arm, "I did no such thing," he said through his teeth, angry and scared at the same time.

"Fine, don't admit that you're a traitor. If you won't tell us why you did it, we'll let Sheena get it out of you," said Belch.

Maximilian didn't need to ask what Sheena would do to him for intentionally misguiding the recovery of the airship. She would have no mercy. He stayed silent, not wanting to give the engineers the satisfaction of a response.

"Let's lock him in the cage." Burp said.

Maximilian started to struggle to get free, but the two hedgehogs were more than he could match, especially now that he had a wounded arm. They were bigger than he was and easily managed to drag him up the back end of the Worm and roughly throw him into the cage, net and all. The metal door slammed shut as Maximilian winced from the pain in his arm.

Burp and Belch went back to their seats and changed course, heading for the dune where they had *actually* buried the Sky-Lion. Maximilian was left to think.

The coyote didn't know what to do; he was wounded and trapped. The evil-engineer hedgehogs knew his true colors. What had he done? Had he really betrayed King Adax? Had he gone crazy?

He had known Anna for less than a day, yet because of her, he had given up everything he had. He had willingly turned on the most powerful and violent figure in the desert. What was he thinking? Somehow, in his heart he knew that Anna was worth the risk. But there was no undoing this choice. He had betrayed his allegiance once again.

"Just like I betrayed the Edges," he mumbled to himself. "Maybe that's all I am, a traitor." Maximilian looked down to his bleeding arm and at the rest of his worn coyote body.

He hated himself.

How could he have ever expected to help Anna? How could he of all people in Highsand, a no good traitor not even loyal to an over-powering king, help the one person who needed the most loyalty, the most trust? He thought of her differently than any other person—someone so pure and innocent, a person who truly deserved loyalty. How could he ever be worthy of the young, brave Captain Anna Tomahawk? He was ashamed of himself.

The only hope, in fact, that Maximilian had left was that somehow, someway Lieutenant Larraby and the Edges would manage to find the Sky-Lion before Burp and Belch.

Suddenly, he remembered Anna was still at his apartment. What had he done! He should've been more careful. He cursed himself for his haphazard decisions with the engineers. Saving the airship wasn't nearly as important as protecting the girl.

He straightened one ear up with his paw. He couldn't give up yet. He still had a chance to redeem himself. If he could only talk his way out of it or escape and get back to Anna, he could explain what went wrong. He could tell her everything he should've told her in the beginning. He would confess everything that happened with the Edges, how he had been coerced into working for King Adax, and even how he had planned to betray her too.

Maybe if he confessed, she would forgive him. It seemed almost as impossible as escaping his capture, but something inside Maximilian told him he had to try.

With his courage renewed, he bit off a piece of his cape and tied it around his arm to make a tourniquet. Then, working his way out of the net with a new determination, he grabbed the bars and stood to watch the approach to the spot where the Sky-Lion lay buried.

The two hedgehogs began digging right away using the appendages attached to the Worm's head. It was loud and rocked the Worm back and forth. The metallic net behind Maximilian clinked loudly against the bars of the cage as the lanterns on the Worm's back creaked and swung against their poles. Through all the noise Maximilian could hardly hear any of the conversation between the hedgehogs, but he did make out one thing:

"The airship is gone!"

Chapter 4

Back at the Edges' hideout, Captain Anna Tomahawk and Lieutenant Larraby sat around a large, oblong table with a dozen or so of the most trusted members of the Edges.

The meeting room was mostly unadorned, evidence of the destitute resources available to the rebellion. None of the chairs matched, and the light was unevenly dispelled from oil lamps in the off-shaped corners. The room was more fit for a nap than a meeting of minds.

The young captain sat patiently in her ripped white tank top. The room was a little too cold and she wished she had her red jacket—even if it was missing a button thanks to the *grouch* in the marketplace the night before. The table was so high it came nearly up to her chin, and the cheery girl had never felt so out of place as she did now, sitting at a conference table in a cave. Everyone had stern faces, and Anna wanted to laugh at their dreadful seriousness.

She gave them as many moments as she could to get quiet and get down to business, but when it wasn't forthcoming, she stood on the chair, put her hands on her hips and started loudly, "What are we talking about exactly?"

The room reacted surprised by her boldness, all eyes turned to her.

Lieutenant Larraby sat at the opposite end of the table, in a much more plush looking chair than she had, Anna noticed. He stood to match her, though, not upon his chair. "The same thing we discussed earlier, Captain—how to fix the airship."

"Ah—" Anna started.

"The Sky-Lion," Larraby quickly corrected himself.

Anna grinned. "Well, what kind of spare parts do you have? You got a scrapyard?"

"I'm afraid not," Larraby answered regretfully. "Resources are limited, we'll have to be creative."

"Not a problem, I'm always creative." Anna said.

"That's good, we will need your ingenuity. But I'm afraid it might not be enough. Even if we were to disassemble many of our inventions and vehicles, it'd be hard to find the necessary components."

"What about the king?" Anna asked seriously, "Does he have scraps we could use?"

"The idea has crossed my mind." Larraby said.

"It's dangerous," said a gray cat from the corner.

"It seems the only option we have," Larraby went on with authority. "In the storehouse at the main garrison there are supplies. But the king won't give them up without a fight, which we obviously want to avoid. We'll have to take them without him knowing. A heist." He announced.

The crowd nodded and mm-hmm'd.

"That's not what I meant. I won't be a part of it," said Anna flatly.

"What do you mean?" the gray cat asked, grooming behind her ear with a paw.

"What do you mean, *Captain*?" Larraby corrected.

Anna winked at him and smiled. "I don't steal."

Larraby raised his hands to the group as if to say, *I'll handle this*. "Captain Anna, we must break into the garrison at Dung Dune City. It's the only place that has the metal needed to repair the airship—the Sky-Lion." He was starting to get the hang of correcting himself before Anna could.

"Oh, that's easy. We'll just ask them to share." She plunked down onto her chair.

The room exchanged glances.

"What is this, some sort of joke?" someone asked.

"Yes, come on, Larraby, what is this all about?"

"Captain Anna, I told you about the king." Someone spit on the ground. "He won't share. This garrison is where the king stores all of his metal—every steamin' spare part for every machine in Dung Dune City. Every gate, every vehicle and weapon, every engine produced by the king and his army comes from this singular metal reserve." Lieutenant Larraby was desperately trying to convince her. "Not to mention that the storehouse sits in the back courtyard of the garrison surrounded by the army's barracks. We can't charge in there and announce ourselves. Stealth is the only advantage we have."

"No it's not, I'm here, and I'm a pretty big advantage, Mr. Lieutenant."

Larraby looked at her, "You are an advantage, but these people won't help you. They've picked their side."

"Yeah, but when they meet me they could change their minds."

"That's a generous thought, Captain. But they won't change."

"You just gotta give people a chance sometimes," Anna said.

The room was quiet.

Larraby finally spoke again, "Not the king, not these people. They're ruthless. Bad. Don't you understand?"

Anna ignored the question, "Well, bad or not, we won't steal from them. I don't want to have to fly the Sky-Lion with stolen parts. She wouldn't be the same. I guess we just have to fix the Sky-Lion another way." She crossed her arms.

"We need those supplies, we have nothing. We have no option but to take them," said someone from her left.

She half-climbed onto the table so she could see who said it and to look them straight in the eye, "No. It's always right to do the right thing. That means, no stealing parts."

As infuriating as it was, it was good logic. No one in the room could argue against that. It was simple and didn't quite accurately appraise the situation, but she had a point. It was always right to do the right thing.

"I admire your character, Captain Anna. But today it's impractical," said Larraby.

"Having character is never impractical."

A couple people in the room sank back into their chairs. Captain Tomahawk's stubbornness was starting to aggravate the group. Larraby could sense it. But he knew that she wouldn't compromise. The Edges would have to find another way to get the supplies needed to repair the Sky-Lion. Stealing them from the king would have been a difficult enough feat on its own, but having to get the supplies honestly would be near impossible.

"What do you recommend, Captain?" asked Larraby.

Anna shrugged. "Like I said before, we ask them nicely." She smiled.

"Larraby, you can't expect us to walk into the king's garrison and *ask* for supplies. They'll know who all of us are, our cover will be blown. The faceless anonymity of our members will be lost," said the cat.

"Lily's right, Anna. There's no going back from this."

"I know, that's fine."

Larraby held the room silent with his contemplative look. "Do you *truly* think this will work, Captain?"

"Yep, why not? Why couldn't they help? You guys kidnapped me and now I'm helping you."

There was a pause while Larraby thought. No one said anything. In spite of all the logical objections there were to Captain Tomahawk's groundless plan, the members sitting at the table could feel in the air that Anna had won over

Larraby. He was going to let her try it and he was going to help her.

It was a terrible idea. To even consider it was a stretch of imagination—a tactical fantasy. It was bold and much more dangerous than a heist would have been. But the girl's conviction had a force attached to it. It made it seem possible, even probable, that it would work. As unlikely a chance for success the idea had, it was as if the simple fact of being on Anna's side insured victory.

"Okay," said Larraby, finally unable to resist the young captain, "we ask...nicely."

"Great!" said Anna.

The rest of the room groaned.

"We send in a small team," Larraby began again, trying to quiet their complaints. "Since they'll recognize many of us, we'll have to go in disguise. Captain Anna will go with us—"

"It's too dangerous to send a little girl." Someone cut him off, obviously frustrated with the plan already.

"Trust me, she can handle herself." He looked at her knowingly, secretly hoping that she wouldn't blurt out that she had out-dueled him. She just smiled at the compliment. Larraby uncomfortably cleared his throat, "We'll need at least four more to load the vehicle. Volunteers?"

The one thing about the Edges was that they were unified. Even if they didn't believe in the exact plan, no one wanted to be excluded from it. It was a chance, however small, at freedom, and it was worth the risk. Almost every hand went up to join the mission.

"Good," said Larraby, proud of the response.

"I want to go," said a tusked boar in a blue jacket seated not far from Anna, "but I have a question."

"Ask your question, Boris," said Larraby.

Boris cracked his neck either way and reached up to rotate a big, gold earing. "I want to make sure I'm understanding *the plan*. We drive into Dung Dune City through the main gate, go straight to the garrison, and ask the guard if he'll give us access to a highly secured vault where we can have our pick from the entire selection of the king's metal supply, then we walk out the front door. That about right?"

"Yep," said Anna. Larraby nodded.

"Sounds crazy. I like it," Boris snorted. Anna winked at him.

Larraby picked another three volunteers for the mission. "We'll leave first thing in the morning. Lily," he said addressing the slim, gray cat, "you're in charge of the disguises."

"Yes sir, Lieutenant," said Lily.

"Dismissed," said Larraby.

"Hey wait, there's one more thing," said Captain Anna. Everyone stopped. "I have to get my sword and pistol back. They're at Max's house."

***

In Highsand, even when a great many good things happen, something bad will always happen too. So, as Captain Tomahawk and the Edges made plans to repair the Sky-Lion, Maximilian Howl was being dragged into a cell in the dungeon of King Adax's palace.

Burp and Belch harshly threw him down. With his hands tied, Maximilian couldn't prevent his head from smacking onto the floor. He let out a small bark, wincing at the impact, and shuddered as his wounded arm sent a bolt of pain through his entire body.

"Don't do this," Maximilian pleaded to the engineers.

"You did this to yourself," said Belch. "Why don't you think about your loyalties for a while?"

"Sheena will be down to see you. *Eventually.*" Burp said menacingly, and the two hedgehogs laughed as they slammed shut the solid-metal, cell door.

Maximilian tried to stand, but his head was spinning and he slumped back down. His canine sense of smell was detecting a dozen atrocious scents from every corner of the prison cell, but he didn't know and didn't want to find out what, exactly, they were coming from. There was no light. Not a window or lamp. Even with his coyote eyesight, he couldn't see in this darkness. He couldn't help but feel intimidated and scared.

What was Sheena going to do to him?

She had always hated Maximilian. Of course, she seemed to hate everything and everyone, but she especially loathed Maximilian. He trembled to think what tortures she would come up with for him. Whatever evils she had in store, he had only one goal—not to give up Anna. He had to protect her. Had to keep her identity a secret.

Was she still at his apartment? What was she doing now? How long had it been, two days? No, it had only been since the morning. Anna wouldn't be expecting him back right away, but how long would she wait before leaving his home? It was hard to keep track of time in the cell. Would she go out looking for him? Would she make it out of the city or be caught by the king's guards? Surely, she knew better than to go wandering around, certainly after what happened in the marketplace the night before. She would be more careful. But then again, she was a very confident young girl. Too much so, Maximilian thought. It got her into trouble. She was brave and strong, but she was only one person and against an army no one would stand a chance. Even if she did make it out into the desert, what would she do? Where would she go? The Edges, they might find her. They would help her. Lieutenant Larraby would help her.

At least, Maximilian hoped that Larraby would help her.

He would recognize her from the night she crashed; he would hear her whole story. He would hear about the jungle. Maximilian bit down hard. Why had he been so stupid that first night in the desert? Why didn't he see Anna immediately for what she was? He had seen her flag, with its green leaf, and her airship. He had heard her stories of the jungle. He even believed them. Why didn't he act on what he knew to be true?

He could've introduced her to Larraby. Of course, Larraby would never have forgiven him for the past. But Larraby would have accepted Anna. She could have helped the Edges. Could've saved them. Now, it was too late.

It was too late for all that, Maximilian thought. He had missed his opportunity to help the Edges and to help Anna. And for what? Why? For one reason: because he was afraid of King Adax. It was all so meaningless now. He had betrayed the beetle anyway.

Maximilian growled at himself on the dungeon floor. He was a coward and a traitor. How could he have been so foolish?

He had to hope that Anna would stay put. For a moment he was thankful that no one in King Adax's army knew where his secret apartment was. Perhaps it was still possible for him to talk his way out of his grim, current predicament. If only Sheena could be reasonable, then he could get back to Anna and they could escape. Or, at least, he could help her escape; the Edges would never let him back on their side, he knew that, but they would accept Anna. They would see the value in having a real pilot, one from the jungle no less.

If only he could get out of the palace.

Slowly his coyote eyes began to adjust to the dark, and he managed to slip out of his binds and tighten the tourniquet around his arm. As Maximilian Howl waited for his captor, the thought of still being able to help his new friend restored his fortitude. Whatever Sheena might do to him, he would persevere.

Chapter 10

"Come here, dear—and stop your wiggling!" said Lily.

"I'm just so excited! Ya know, for a cat you really know a lot about disguises, don't you?" asked Anna.

"Yes," Lily paused contemplatively; she leaned back and her gray fur shimmered in the lamplight. "We've been hiding for a long time." She tied a final knot across Captain Anna's back, cinching it tight, "That's it. You're all set, dear."

"Thanks!" said Anna as she spun a few times and turned to look in the mirror.

She was disguised as an old lady, complete with a yellow cowl that drooped down past her eyes. It would've been impossible to hide the young spark in her eyes, so Lily thought it best to hide them entirely in the shadow. As a finishing touch, Lily gave her a walking stick and a little basket to accentuate the disguise.

"I look so sneaky!"

"That's the opposite of what you want, my dear. As long as you don't go skipping down the road, you'll look inconspicuous. They wouldn't be able to tell you apart from Sheena herself."

"Who's that?"

Lily showed a toothy feline grin. "An old woman who works for the king. She's quite nasty."

"Well, *I'm* going to be a nice old woman."

"Seems you already are," they both giggled.

"Are you two finished?" Lieutenant Larraby was leaning in the doorway, wearing a tight green shirt that didn't suit him. He had tucked his yellow beard into the shirt and donned a scarf high around his face to hide the rest of it.

"Yes, sir," said Lily.

"Ready!" said Anna.

All of the other people for the mission were ready and waiting in the main chamber of the Edges' hideout. A crowd had gathered around them to wish them luck and see them off. The volunteers were beyond recognition from the day before, except that is, for Boris. It was hard to conceal his visage. His tusks were polished and shining white.

Lily walked over to Boris and gave him a cat-like kiss on the cheek. "Be careful."

"I'll be back before you notice I'm gone." Boris took Lily's soft paw and put it against his coarse face. She nuzzled against him and purred.

"Just be careful."

A few people hugged the other volunteers and they all stepped back.

"If we don't return by nightfall," Larraby instructed, "contact the spies in the palace. If they inform you that Captain Anna's alive, come for her. Otherwise…" Larraby let the word hang. There would be no rescues. "She's the only hope we have." He looked to her like she was a prize.

The crowd silently acknowledged their leader's instructions.

Anna set her face seriously, understanding how dangerous it was, and how much the Edges needed her. How much they needed this mission to succeed. "Don't worry about us," she said. "I'll do all the talking, and we'll be just fine."

"To the edge," Larraby saluted.

"And the farthest shore," the group responded.

They waved a few more times and started up the ladder towards the cave entrance. In the lobby of the cave was a metal door. Anna hadn't noticed it before, because the light was so poor in the cave. But now, with the morning sun shining, it stuck out rather sorely.

"What's in there?" she asked.

"Our ride," Boris said dryly.

Lieutenant Larraby pulled a lever that was concealed from view behind a boulder, and the wall came alive with weathered gears and metalworking. Wondrous sounds came from the clinking and clanging of metal on metal wheels connecting together. The door slowly collapsed down on itself, folding in half again and again until it was but a few inches off the ground and formed a sort of platform in front of a small garage.

Larraby walked into the darkness of the room.

Suddenly a roar came from inside, not that of an animal but of a machine springing to technological life. It was a familiar sound to Captain Anna Tomahawk. It was the sound of an engine. Orange wires that wrapped around the front and top of the vehicle started to glow, just like the radio that Larraby had shown Anna earlier, and a shape started to form out of the darkness underneath the illumination.

The sound it made was so similar to that of the Sky-Lion, that for a split second Anna thought it might be an airship. Her breath got caught in her throat, but then the vehicle lurched forward.

It was strangely shaped. There was a main cabin on top, with room for four or five passengers, and a steering wheel in the front. An empty storage bed in the back hung near the ground. It had a metal tread that Anna knew, looking at it for just a split second, must rotate around like a wheel to propel it forward. A furnace and a steam tank were concealed underneath. There were knobs and gears sticking out every which way, and to Anna, it looked incomplete. Like it hadn't finished being made before it started being used. But nonetheless, it was impressive.

Most interestingly, it had a long arm out to the side that had a seat hanging from it. The seat was almost as low to the ground as the metal tread. Attached was a giant fan.

Someone leaned over Anna's shoulder to whisper in her ear, "Impressed?"

"I want to drive it!"

"I know you say you're the greatest pilot in the world, but I'll be driving, Captain," Larraby cut in with a smirk. He strapped his goggles on. "Everyone in."

The other five, including Anna, hopped aboard the vehicle.

"What do you call it!?" Anna asked over the thrum of the engine.

"The Duster!" Larraby yelled back. "We don't take it out much, runs on steam!"

"So does the Sky-Lion!"

Larraby nodded. "Hold on!"

The Duster shot out of the cave with incredible speed, much faster than Anna was anticipating. It threw her back into her seat, and whipped her yellow hood down onto her shoulders.

She shouted with enjoyment at going so fast as she spun all around to take in the ride. When she looked to her right she saw Boris sitting at the end of the arm and operating controls for the giant fan. It was blowing sand from the side of the Duster over the tracks behind them, instantly hiding the path. "Hey, that's really smart!" she yelled to Larraby.

"Watch!" he shouted over his shoulder.

As if on cue, Boris pulled a lever and the extended arm and his seat launched in an arc over to the opposite side of the Duster, where they settled with a bounce. He began to blow sand from the other side of the vehicle. Then he pulled the lever back once again and arched back over the center of the Duster to land on its left side again. He continued to bounce back and forth in the seat over the vehicle, working to cover their tracks and blowing sand from every direction.

"I don't want to drive anymore—I want to do that!"

"If we make it out of the city alive, I'll have Boris show you," Larraby promised.

Anna leaned forward over his seat and shoulder, and gave him a kiss on the cheek. "I could figure it out!"

Larraby blushed at the girl's affection.

It wasn't long before they arrived at Dung Dune City. The main gate was a giant steel door, painted black with a threatening scorpion designed into the metal. They had to go through the main entrance in order to bring the Duster.

Entering Dung Dune City from the main road was a different experience altogether than when Maximilian had brought her to the city. This road was a straight shot up to King Adax's palace. A few protective walls and gates were in the way, but otherwise the view was spectacular, albeit rather menacing. There were scorpions sculpted and carved and painted into and onto what felt like everything.

The young captain was watching everything roll by with her eyes and mouth wide open. Someone reached from behind her and put her cowl back over to hide her undisguised hair. The cowl covered her eyes and she had to push it back up a little in order to see out. There was so much to look at. There were people everywhere along the sides of the road looking at the Duster as it passed. Little did they know, that they were looking at Lieutenant Larraby and a selection of other notable rebels. Boris was riding the Duster's arm arched high in the air—like a scorpion's tail, Anna thought.

"We're drawing a lot of attention, Lieutenant." Boris called down from his seat.

Larraby didn't acknowledge him. He knew they would attract unwanted notice, but they couldn't slow down. They had to get to the garrison quickly. Well, as quickly as they could after making just one stop. It was the only acceptable delay, and it had been carefully planned—retrieving Anna's sword and pistol. The Duster came grinding to a halt just before an intersection of dusty, stone streets.

"Here, out." Larraby commanded.

A girl, looking just a few years older than Anna, tapped the captain on the shoulder. "Follow me."

She jumped down off the Duster and started walking towards an alleyway. Anna spryly followed her, starting to run. A few bystanders caught a glimpse of her jumping from the top of the Duster to the ground. They paused to inspect a little further.

"Anna," Larraby called, she turned. "Remember, you're *very* old. Take it slow." He arched his eyebrows toward the people on the street.

"Right!" she said and leaned on her walking stick as she slowly turned to follow the girl.

The rest of the Edges on the Duster sat back nervously, trying to look nonchalant.

"How do you know where to go?" Anna asked the girl once they'd turned the corner.

"I live here. Shhh, we have to be quiet."

Anna hunched her shoulders, trying to stay in character.

"It's not far at all." The girl whispered as they turned another corner.

At the far end of the alleyway a pair of soldiers turned towards them, wearing the red capes and scorpion insignias of the king's army.

"In here," Captain Anna said and pulled the girl back into a shadowed doorway. The two girls pressed close together in the shadows, their faces almost touching. They could hear the soldiers talking and walking towards them.

"It's about time he got what was coming to him."

Anna recognized the voice—the one-eyed Colonel from the marketplace—the grouch who had tried to steal her ruby pendant!

"Agreed, that stupid coyote should've known better than to double cross the king," said the other soldier.

"Coyote? Max!" Anna squeaked. The girl clapped a hand over Anna's mouth.

"Well, it'll be his last time double-crossing anyone. Once Sheena's finished with him, he won't be doing much of anything."

"What was it all about?"

"I'm not sure, some secret the engineers are keeping. The real shame is that Sheena's got the coyote all to herself. I wish I could tear a piece out of that mongrel. I never liked him."

As the two walked by, Anna, the Captain of the Sky-Lion and the meanest-dueling, quickest-shooting pilot there ever was, had to use all her willpower to stop herself from jumping out in front of the two men and demanding that they tell her where Maximilian was being kept.

She had it in her heart to confront them immediately, but she didn't. For all her naivety in a thousand other situations, she always made the best choice in a crisis. She knew that now was not the time for a confrontation, even as she was already planning to save her friend.

When the soldiers left the alley the two girls ducked out from within the doorway and sprinted towards Maximilian's apartment. They arrived to find the front door still locked from when Maximilian had left Anna to meet with the king. So they slipped into the next alley that came around the back of the apartment. Nothing had changed since Anna was last there. The window was still broken from when Lieutenant Larraby had kidnapped her. Even the spider web was still in the corner.

Maximilian never came back for her.

Anna, always thinking the best, figured that her coyote friend must have been captured before he could return. She climbed inside through the window while the other girl kept watch.

"Yes!" Anna shouted as she leapt over the couch. "Still here!" She rolled up her yellow cloak past her waist and strapped on her belt, slipping her sword through its sheath and holstering her pistol. She fitted her pack over her head across her body.

"Did you find them?" the girl asked through the window.

"Yep! Got 'em," Anna said happily, slinging her red jacket over her other shoulder.

"Let's go, they can't wait for us for long."

"Right." Anna started to climb back out the window. In her rush, she didn't notice it happen, but her yellow cloak got caught on a broken piece of glass in the window frame. It ripped a small tear underneath her arm, and as the two ran away from the apartment, a piece of yellow cloth remained fluttering in the wind on the spike of glass.

CHapTeR 11

When the girls made it back to the Duster, there was a small crowd of people surrounding it. Although the group from the Edges was hardly recognizable, the Duster was in and of itself an outlaw. There were those who would know what it was and who it belonged to. It wouldn't be long before someone recognized the vehicle.

They had to move fast.

Thankfully, the two girls were small and could squeeze through the crowd easily. As they climbed back aboard the Duster, Lieutenant Larraby looked down over his shoulder to them. The girl gave him a quick nod to confirm that she and Captain Anna had found the weapons. It was all the confirmation Larraby needed, and he started the Duster rolling forward again.

The crowd spread like water around a rock as the Duster slowly pushed up the street.

Captain Anna felt much more equipped for whatever was going to happen now that she had her sword and pistol again. In fact, the entire group seemed to take a collective breath of relief once the self-proclaimed mighty, little girl was again armed and dangerous.

"We're almost there. Be ready for anything," Larraby warned.

Boris unstrapped himself from the Duster's arm and dropped down into the main cabin with a heavy thud. Everyone in the group pulled their jackets down and tight. Anna made sure the yellow hood draped low over her face.

"Captain Tomahawk, up here with me," Lieutenant Larraby said.

He was a good leader, and since she didn't know where they were going, Anna thought it best not to argue with him about giving orders, even though she did outrank him. She climbed over the back of the seat to sit next to the bearded lieutenant.

"Make sure that hood is low."

"Right," said Anna, "I'll do the talking. Did you know they have Max?"

"What?" asked Larraby, his tone gruff.

"They have Max. I don't know why, but he's in the dungeon somewhere, we overheard a guy in the alley. He's a prisoner, Lar!"

Lieutenant Larraby shot her a doubtful look. He wasn't concerned at all about Maximilian Howl's capture, the coyote was a no-good traitor as far as he cared. He *was* concerned, however, about Anna "doing the talking." She could be a rather loose end when it came to conversation, and he wasn't entirely sure she was capable of disguising her voice and staying in character. Larraby knew that most likely, everything hinged on the disguises working as he planned.

The idea of asking for supplies from the king's garrison felt like less than half-brained, but if it was going to work, it would be a miracle, and the miracle would be entirely because of Captain Anna. She had already proven herself as a fighter, and in their strategy planning she had proved she could be convincing, but those facts did little to calm Larraby's nerves. He had to hope she could pull it off. Cooperation was his only choice, if they wanted her help.

Anna butted in before he had a chance to respond, "We'll go save him after we get the supplies."

Larraby rolled his eyes.

"Don't worry so much, Lar. I'm the greatest adventurer there ever was. It'll work!"

What will work? Asking for supplies or rescuing the traitor? But Larraby kept his thoughts to himself and only answered her with a nod. He didn't say anything about being called Lar either. In fact, he kind of liked it.

The Duster pulled right up to the gate of the garrison. It was flooded with the king's soldiers. They were absolutely everywhere.

"That's a lot of soldiers," said Anna.

"Stop!" yelled a guard at the gate. "What's going on here, you can't bring that thing through here. There are troops in the courtyard, you'll run them over."

"Good," Boris said from behind Anna. Larraby punched him hard in the shin between the seats. Anna snickered.

Only the top of the brave captain's hood stuck out higher than the front shield of the Duster, and without changing her voice at all, in truth, she didn't even attempt to sound old or stay in character. She simply and flatly said, "We have to get to the metals storehouse inside."

The guard laughed as another guard joined him. "I'm sure you do, and who might you be?"

Anna huffed, "Who might I be?"

Oh, no, thought Larraby, *here she goes.* And Lieutenant Larraby did, indeed, fully expect her to launch into her long-winded introduction—all of that business about being the meanest-dueling and quickest-shooting *pilot* there ever was.

"Don't you recognize me?" Anna said indignantly as she stood. Larraby reached for his sword on the floor. Boris clenched his fists.

When the two guards saw her, they immediately dropped their heads in a bow. "I'm so sorry, forgive me for not recognizing your voice," the guard pleaded.

Everyone aboard the Duster looked around at one another puzzled. Everyone except Larraby, he understood.

"Please," the guard continued, "let me get the troops out of the courtyard, then you can go through right away. Take whatever you need."

"That's great, thanks!" said Anna excitedly. Too excitedly.

The Edges aboard the Duster nervously gulped and waited for the reaction.

The guards looked back and forth to one another, heads still bowed. They raised curious eyebrows at the exuberant thank you. "Of course...Sheena."

Sheena? thought Anna, *Wait! The disguise!* It really was as good as Lily had said after all. "I'm not—"

Larraby quickly pulled Anna back into the seat before she could get out her words and slapped a hand over her mouth.

"Sorry, did you say something, Sheena?" said the guard from the ground below.

"Carry on," Lieutenant Larraby instructed, still holding Anna's mouth shut and giving her a serious look.

She shrugged underneath him.

The guards quickly bowed again and rushed off into the courtyard. In a matter of minutes the entire area was free and clear of all soldiers. The storehouse doorway was being opened across the way and somehow, they had done all of it without drawing a single sword or firing a single shot.

Lieutenant Larraby drove the Duster right up against the entranceway and turned it around. Pulling some gears he started going in reverse. The bed of the Duster fit perfectly between the two sides of the doorway.

"It can go backward too?" Anna asked.

"Of course." Larraby said trying to hurry and climb down the side of the Duster.

"The Sky-Lion can only go forward."

"The Sky-Lion can't go anywhere, Captain, unless we get out of here. We're not done yet." He took another step down the side, his mechanical leg ticking beneath his baggy disguise.

"Well, come on," Anna said as she outpaced the lieutenant's climb by sliding down the bed in the back. She jumped when she reached the bottom, limberly landing on her feet and bursting into a run, "I'll show you what I need!" she shouted over her shoulder.

Lieutenant Larraby rubbed the bridge of his nose and sighed as he followed her. The rest of the group was already inside rummaging around the scraps of metal.

Anna was turning every direction, pointing and saying, "This. This. This. This and that and one of these!"

The team around her had to hustle to keep up with her instructions as they loaded everything into the Duster.

"Those pipes," she said, "That curved plate—ooh!—some of those latched valves too!"

Larraby started to wonder if she was going to point at everything.

As she was shouting out which pieces to load, one of the guards who had let them in walked around the corner of the Duster to stand inside with them. The group slowed down, even Anna, when they saw him.

"Anything I can do to help?" he sounded suspicious.

"No," said Larraby, "We're almost finished, isn't that right, *Sheena*?"

Anna didn't respond to being called Sheena, she was too distracted by the metal pieces and parts lying around.

"We're almost finished," Larraby repeated to assure the guard.

The guard looked over at the yellow-cloaked figure. She was moving so easily, like she was but a young girl. He had only seen Sheena in person once before, but he didn't remember or imagine her moving with such athleticism. Just then, as Anna was reaching up for a part hanging on the wall, she pinched her leg against some sharp metal and the rip in her cloak underneath her arm tore right down to her knee as she stretched. The guard saw her white sleeveless shirt, her fitted boots and—a young girls body!—they'd been duped!

Everyone paused at the same time. They all looked at the guard.

He looked at them.

Knowing the game was up, Larraby undid his scarf, and pulled his yellow beard out from underneath his shirt.

The guard recognized him immediately. A panic spread across his face as he looked around at each of them again, he suddenly recognized all of them. He spun quickly and started to shout, "Sound the—!" But he didn't quite get it all out before Boris knocked him hard with a hoofed hand on the top of his head, shutting him up and dropping him to the floor.

"I know the girl likes to shop, but, Larraby, we got to get out of here," said Boris.

"Captain, let's move!"

"One last thing—we need that!" Anna pointed along the wall to a giant piece of metal. It was almost as large as the entire bed of the Duster.

"We can't, there's no steamin' time!"

"I can't fix the Sky-Lion without it, we have to have that piece!"

Boris, Larraby, and the others all rushed over to the wall where the piece of sheet metal was leaning. It must've weighed over a thousand pounds. It took all of them together to drag it off the wall. On top of that, the process made an alarming amount of noise. Other scraps were falling and grinding against one another, it sounded like an eruption of pots and pans.

The team had just managed to lean the oversized sheet of metal against the bed of the Duster, when a loud alarm started to sound. "Hurry!" someone shouted. They all pushed hard to lodge the metal securely onto the back of the Duster.

"Get in!" Larraby commanded. The team jumped into the back. "Where's Anna?" He looked around in a panic.

"Up here!" She called down from the main cabin, "Hold on!"

No one in the Duster had ever seen Anna steer or fly or control anything, but they knew without a doubt, that she would be a wild and fast driver. They all braced themselves against the scraps for a bumpy ride.

On the balconies inside the storehouse, soldiers started pouring in through the doors. They started down the stairs, like a waterfall of red capes. When they reached the bottom, they broke into a run across the large room, headed straight for the back of the Duster. The group was defenseless, all their weapons were in the cabin with Anna, and they still weren't moving.

The soldiers were getting closer.

Anna peeked over the back a second time, "Larraby, which one is forward again?"

"Beneath the seat—hurry!"

"Got it!" she climbed back over the seats into the front. Switched the lever beneath the seat all the way around and cranked the wheel hard, the Duster roared to life.

The soldiers were almost there!

"Hold on!" Anna yelled, and she threw back her hood. The duster was so overloaded with metal scraps that it started all too slowly. Soldiers were everywhere trying to run alongside the Duster and climb aboard. Anna swerved back and forth to keep them at bay, forcing them to jump aside to avoid getting run over.

The steam-powered vehicle started to pick up speed, as Larraby and some of the others climbed up the back of the bed and into the main cabin.

Soldiers were shutting the main gate out of the garrison's courtyard. Anna looked carelessly back over her shoulder as she steered. She found Larraby's eyes, "I'm gonna ram it!"

"Break through it!" Larraby yelled in agreement as he sat down in the seat beside her and held on.

"Here we go!"

Everyone in the Duster ducked as they slammed into the gate. The noise was like an explosion, breaking the gates off their hinges and slamming them to the ground like a drawbridge dropped too fast.

Dust and debris flew up in every direction as the Duster bounced hard over the gate.

"Take it easy in the street!" Larraby shouted.

Anna steered towards the main road, keeping the speed just faster than the soldiers could run. The Duster was making all kinds of unusual, broken-sounding noises. It didn't sound like it was going to make it. Half the steam valves on the right side had been scraped off as they had plowed through the gate. The whole vehicle was getting unbearably hot as the remaining valves worked overtime to compensate.

Everyone aboard the vehicle scampered to the opposite side of the overheating steam valves to avoid getting burned, or worse, if the pipes burst.

The noise the Duster was making frightened everyone out of the way and into the alleyways and onto the side streets off the main road. Now it was a straight shot out of Dung Dune City.

They'd made it!

They tore out of the main entrance to the city, and started to pick up speed in the open desert.

"Boris, on the fan!" Lieutenant Larraby commanded.

But Boris was nowhere to be found.

CHapTeR 12

Boris had, in fact, fallen out of the back of the Duster much earlier without notice. As Anna had pulled violently out of the storehouse, he had lost his grip. Hooves are not as easy to hold on with as hands, even for an extra-skilled boar like Boris. He had simply bounced out.

By the time he dusted himself off and stood up, he was already surround by a dozen soldiers. They seized him before he could quite figure out what had happened or get his senses back about him.

Still, Boris fought, struggling to get free, or at least to make it as difficult as possible for the soldiers to transport him. A whole squad of escorts was needed, some five soldiers, to literally drag him through the streets.

When they got him outside the garrison, a

caged vehicle was waiting for them. They shoved him inside and locked it securely.

"Take him to Sheena," instructed one soldier. "This is Boris the Brute, he's part of the rebellion." Of course the soldiers and everyone in King Adax's employ always called the Edges "the rebellion" because they hated to acknowledge the Edges by their name. They hated it because it so accurately spoke of what they believed in—that there was an edge, and therefore a place beyond the desert, a place better than the desert.

"Go ahead and take me to Sheena, you pigs!" which was somewhat amusing coming from a boar. "I'm not scared of any of you. Take me to the king himself if you want." Boris spit on the ground.

"That's enough out of you," said a soldier, who then tried to stab Boris through the cage. Boris grabbed the spear just past the head and broke it in half between the bars. But before he could do anything with it the soldier yelled, "Get him out of here!"

The steam powered vehicle slowly clicked away towards the palace, a dozen legs moving like a giant mechanical bug. The swaying back and forth as the cage wobbled made Boris nauseated, and when they entered the palace dungeon, he was still too dizzy to put up a fight. The soldiers hadn't taken any chances this time though. They had plenty of help to bind him and throw him into a cell.

Boris was standing again as soon as he hit the ground, popping up with ferocity and charging the metal door. He banged as hard as he could against it with his fist. "You can stop me, but you can't stop all of us!"

There was a terrible stench coming from the dry and dusty cell, but he couldn't figure out which direction it was coming from.

At least I know where the door is, he thought. It was so dark in the cell he couldn't see anything. "I'll run you through when I get out of here!" Boris began slamming at the door until he lost track of time and worked up a sweat. With heaving sighs he jerked open the collar of his blue jacket, slumping to the ground against the door. He gave a low grunt, and punched the ground, defeated.

As he finally sat in the silence, he heard a voice.

"Hello? Is someone there? If you can hear my voice, call out."

Boris laid down flat in front of the door to get his ear as close as possible to the doorframe. "Who's there?"

"My name is Maximilian Howl, I'm—" Maximilian was going to include his formal title, but now that he'd betrayed the king he wasn't really anything or anybody important, just a miserable coyote who knew too much for his own good.

"Maximilian? What are you doing in here?" Boris asked, shocked to hear a familiar voice.

"Boris?"

"Yes, it's me! Are you guarding my cell? You traitor!"

"No, no, I'm…I'm locked up."

"Locked up? What'd you do now?"

"It's a long story, there's a girl, a Captain—"

"Anna," Boris cut him off.

"Yes, yes! Is she all right? Is she with you?"

"Of course she's not with me. She's fine…I think…as far as I know."

"What are you saying, as far as you know?" Maximilian demanded.

"She and the others were making their getaway from the garrison. We had to get supplies for," Boris hesitated, carefully picking his words in case someone was listening, "for—something about repairing a *vehicle*. I got left behind." Boris didn't want to embarrass himself by admitting he fell out of the Duster.

So Anna has joined up with the Edges, Maximilian thought. He smiled to himself for the first time since he had split ways with her. Larraby would help her. Then he remembered where he was. "I am sorry, old friend," Maximilian said sincerely, knowing that whatever was in store for the both of them would be truly horrible.

"We're not friends, Howl. You betrayed us. You betrayed all of us."

"I know. I know I did."

They were both quiet for a while.

"What will she do if she repairs the ship?" Maximilian finally asked to break the silence.

"Leave, probably. Why would she stay in Highsand if all that stuff she says about the jungle is true?"

"It is true," Maximilian said confidently.

"You seem to like her," said Boris.

Maximilian thought about it for a moment, "She's the best. She's all I have."

"Yeah. For what it's worth, she vouched for you. I was there when she told Larraby. She said you changed."

"What does it matter now if I have changed? We're caught."

"Eh. I'm not so sure."

"What do you mean?"

"Oh," Boris cleared his throat, "I'm fairly certain I can break this door down. Just wouldn't have anywhere to go once I did. The palace is swarming with guards."

"You'll just break through?" Maximilian asked skeptically.

"Sure, no door can hold Boris the Brute," Boris replied. "This door would be the easy part. If we did manage to make it outside, it would be best to wait until it's dark for our escape. We've got a few hours till sunset."

"No, we mustn't delay. I'm not sure how long I've been in here—almost a day, I estimate. But Sheena still hasn't been to see me. She could be here any moment."

"So, it's now or never?"

Maximilian's silence answered the boar's question.

"What if your door is thicker than my door?"

Maximilian rapped on the door with his knuckles, listening to the sound. "We'll have to risk it. I can show you the way out of here. I know the palace and the city better than anyone. If we can get outside, we can get back to the Edges."

"I would never take you back. You can't be trusted. For all I know, this is all a trick," said Boris sternly.

Maximilian realized that Boris wasn't going to change his mind about him anytime soon, but they did need one another. "Fair enough, but you need me, Boris."

There was a contemplative pause before Boris grunted, "Yeah."

It got quiet.

"Boris?"

Nothing.

"Boris?" Maximilian asked, searching with his voice.

Maximilian's call was answered by a loud crash and then another and then the sound of metal grating rapidly against stone and a thud.

"Told you." Boris stood, dusting off his clothes. "I'm out," he said flatly. "Stand back."

Maximilian scooted away from the door, and just in time. With a running step Boris crashed through in one blow. Maximilian looked up at his hulking form as he straightened to stand in the doorway. Boris was a silhouette as the opening let in a soft orange light from down the hall. Maximilian squinted having been in the dark for so long, and Boris' tusks glinted in the light.

"They're going to need some new doors," the brute said.

Maximilian stood up and took a cautious step towards the dangerous creature. His injury, combined with his state of being unarmed, didn't give him any comfort as he came nearer to Boris the Brute. And he had not the slightest guess whether Boris was to be trusted either. Or if he would simply snap him in half like he did the doors.

When Maximilian stepped close enough for the light to fall on him, Boris's face changed to a scowl. "You're hurt. You didn't tell me you were hurt."

"It didn't come up," Maximilian joked.

Boris grunted. "Alright, but don't let it slow you down. You've got to lead the way. I don't want to get lost with all those creepy statues everywhere."

Maximilian nodded and slowly stepped past Boris, careful not to accidentally touch him. He took a few steps down the hall and turned back. "There will be guards."

Boris smirked. "Can't wait."

The two escapees sneaked down the hallway towards the lamp as quietly as they could. Maximilian's padded feet making less noise than a falling leaf, while Boris' hooves clumped loudly on the sand dusted stone. Maximilian turned back to him exasperated at the excessive noise and gave him a disapproving look.

"We're trying to be quiet," Maximilian said sarcastically.

"Sorry," Boris mouthed as he shrugged a goofy, silent apology.

When they got to the end of the hall, they had no idea what to expect—a single guard, a dozen guards? It was a wild guess either way. This could quickly turn into a bad idea if they weren't careful. But as they peeked around the corner towards the stairwell that led up and out of the dungeon, they were alone.

There was no one.

Not a single soldier of the king to keep an eye on the two most important prisoners they'd seen in years. It was too good to be true. They bolted across the open room towards the stairwell and started climbing as fast as they could. They stopped on the landing at the top behind a metal door.

"When we go out the door, take a sharp right, then down the hall and take your second left, and run towards the portrait of the king, then another right and there's a window to the roof. We'll have to find our way down from there."

"Got it," Boris confirmed.

Maximilian was about to open the door when Boris stopped him. "I'll go first," he said.

The coyote wasn't about to argue with him, Boris would have to break through the window anyway so he would need to be in front.

Boris cracked the door ever so slightly and they listened.

Further away they could hear someone's boot heels clicking on the stone floor, but the noise was fading away rather than building towards them. They looked to one another for confirmation, and with a shrug and arched brows they swung open the door. They turned the sharp right just as Maximilian had instructed, and took the corner on the second left, but there was no portrait to run towards. In its place, at the end of the hallway, were Sheena and a wall of guards calmly walking towards them.

Maximilian swirled gracefully and came to a halt while Boris sort of skidded as he slowed his stomping run. He punched the wall hard in frustration. "Dead end."

"Back the other way!" Maximilian said and turned around.

Boris followed right behind him.

"Stop them," Sheena's withered mouth said calmly from underneath her yellow, hooded robe. Two-dozen guards broke into a chase.

"Which way!?" Boris shouted at the coyote.

"Left!" Maximilian said as he came up tightly on a turn.

Unable to slow down enough to get a clean turn, Boris crashed into the wall as he rounded the corner. A beetle statue spilled from its stand and shattered on the ground.

"Hurry!" Maximilian shouted back to him, now putting significant ground ahead of the slow boar. Even with an injured arm Maximilian was still much faster than the blue-jacketed brute.

Boris couldn't run fast enough. He could hear the guards gaining on him. Even being the mighty warrior that he was, Boris the Brute could feel panic setting in. His legs felt ineffectual and detached, like trying to run in a dream. He looked back over his shoulder and saw at the front of the pack behind him was a particularly fast, black-tailed jackrabbit.

Boris recognized him right away, Albert—one of the best sharpshooters in the king's army. He tried to will his legs to move faster.

Maximilian was already to the end of the hall, waiting at a set of double doors for Boris. He could see the group of soldiers chasing now less than thirty yards behind. In the front of the chasing horde, Maximilian too, spotted Albert.

Spotted the miniaturized rifle strapped across his back.

Spotted the cold, heartless look in his eyes, and watched as the black-tailed jackrabbit spun the gun around, took aim, and pulled the trigger.

Boris the Brute stumbled a few steps and fell at Maximilian's feet.

Chapter 13

Captain Anna Tomahawk, Lieutenant Larraby, and company had pushed the Duster to its limits to make their getaway from Dung Dune City. They had driven straight to the new location for the Sky-Lion. The airship had been moved to the far side of a large dune right outside the Edges' base. The dune was high enough to hide it from any wandering desert scouts and far enough away from Dung Dune City or any nearby villages to keep the secret reconstruction of the Sky-Lion safe. The trip had been a quiet one as they thought of Boris. Had he been captured?

Was he even still alive?

When they arrived at the site, Captain Anna was pleased to see that despite still being broken beyond recognition, the Sky-Lion was at least sitting with all its original pieces and parts salvaged from the crash-site. She had made sure to point out at the garrison more than enough parts for the total repair of the airship. In fact, she had done well more than that. She had directed the team at the garrison to get enough pieces to expand the Sky-Lion to add capacity for as many as ten additional passengers.

In all her life, she had never tried to make the Sky-Lion bigger than it already was. Its two-person capacity was more than enough for her lone adventures through the jungle. But now that she needed to transport a different kind of cargo, a living cargo of people, she knew she needed to make adjustments. Her quick thinking in the garrison had secured the parts, and now the rebuilding could begin.

Yet, there was another more pressing matter on her mind than the rebuilding of the Sky-Lion. Something that mattered to her even more than the airship she adored so much.

Maximilian Howl.

Ever since she had overheard the guard in the alleyway, she'd been thinking about him. She wasn't worried, Captain Anna never worried, but rather she was mentally planning a breakout. Or, at least, committing to break him out. How, she wasn't quite sure.

She knew that whatever he had done, she could forgive. It was part of her personal code—once a friend of Captain Anna Tomahawk, always a friend. She wasn't about to give up on Maximilian when he needed her the most. She was a hero, and to give up on him, would go against all her heroic positions.

It simply wasn't an option.

She was thinking this very thing, in fact, when Lieutenant Larraby approached her. "Well, Captain, the parts are all here. What's the first order of business?" Lieutenant Larraby had intentionally pushed thoughts of Boris out of his mind, trying to prioritize the most crucial needs. The two looked out at the wreckage of the Sky-Lion, all the new raw materials scattered about.

"We go back for Max and Boris."

"No, that's out of the question. Boris understood that the mission was dangerous. He was prepared to risk his freedom and even his life to gather these steamin' parts. I won't have his loss wasted. Maximilian will get what he deserves."

"I already told you, Lar—Max is a good guy. We have to go back! We can't leave them. No matter what."

"Boris is beyond our help, and Maximilian is none of our concern, even if he is a friend of *yours*." Larraby wasn't about to compromise. A group was starting to gather around them to listen in on the young girl's conversation with their leader.

"A friend of mine is a friend worth saving," Anna said seriously. "I'll go back for him myself," and she turned towards the crowd to leave.

"No," Larraby responded quickly, turning her around, "we need your help here. Fixing the airship is the only way."

Captain Tomahawk glared at him. She didn't like being ordered around. "Listen up," Anna marched towards Larraby, doing her best to get in his face, "I outrank you," she said poking him in the chest. "I don't need anybody's help to save Max and Boris. You all need me, remember?" She looked at the crowd over Larraby's shoulder. "You wouldn't even have a chance without me. I'm the pilot. See this?" Anna held up her ruby pendant, "I can do anything as long as I have this. I can walk right into Dung Dune City and walk out with Max and Boris."

"What do you mean you can do *anything*?"

"Anything good."

Lieutenant Larraby was confused and momentarily speechless. He had never seen the young captain act so sternly, and he recognized that he had clearly over-stepped a boundary, still he couldn't give up so easily.

"Regardless of what you can and can't do, we need you more than the coyote or Boris."

"Everybody needs me."

"Captain, they might already be dead." Larraby said.

"Then we gotta hurry!"

"Anna, I know you think you can take on the king's army alone, but—"

"I can, that's what you don't get. You're not listening to me. No one stands a chance against me. I'm the greatest, Larraby. I can't lose!"

The bearded lieutenant shook his head in frustration. "Even if you did manage to rescue them, where would you go? Would you walk the desert all the way back here? Give away the location of our hideout? There would be a steamin' army on your heels the whole way."

"Well, you don't know how good I am at rescue missions. I could do it," Anna said. "Why don't you believe me?"

"Belief has nothing to do with it."

Anna just stared back at him.

She knew that Larraby was too stubborn to change his mind. The lieutenant thought his plan was better than hers. It didn't matter what she was capable of or how she had proven herself, he could see no other way of doing things but his own.

"Listen to him, dear," Lily said, coming up behind Anna. "I know you could save them. But why not use the Sky-Lion? That's why we risked everything to get parts to fix the ship. That's why Boris went in the first place." Lily sat down on her hind paws as if her next point was so final it didn't require standing. "Don't waste his sacrifice."

"If we don't have a working airship and a way out of Highsand, then we don't have anything. Those two will be okay for a while," Larraby said. "The king will want them alive to talk. But, Captain, you must show us the way out of Highsand, with or without them. We're all counting on you to lead us out of this steamin' desert."

Anna took a deep breath as she considered the words. It was in her personal code to never change her mind when she was right, and she was right. She could succeed with a lone rescue, on foot if she had to. It would be dangerous and difficult, but nevertheless possible. She could do anything after all. But so many responsibilities had been placed on her now.

The conversation had put her at odds with Lieutenant Larraby, the friendly gray cat, and no doubt countless others standing in the crowd listening. She wanted to make peace.

The Sky-Lion wasn't the only way to stage an escape, but it was a good way. The king's troops wouldn't be able to surround an aircraft like they had the Duster. Not to mention, that the Sky-Lion seemed like the only way that didn't require a battle.

But the only way *to what* was the real question now. To saving Maximilian? To getting back to the jungle? To showing the Edges the way out of Highsand? Or to simply wasting time while Maximilian and Boris needed help?

"I want you to make me a promise," the girl said at last.

Larraby looked at her, tucking his chin towards his shoulder. "What is it?"

"I want you to promise that if I fix the Sky-Lion, the Edges will forgive Max."

The crowd scoffed and mumbled amongst themselves.

Larraby's face grew even more serious. "You don't understand what you're asking."

"It doesn't matter how hard it is or what he did. If somebody wants to change and wants forgiveness, they should have a chance."

Larraby waited for her to explain more, to say something further. On some level, he almost wanted to be convinced of what she was saying, but that was all she offered, a simple explanation for a very complex situation. It wasn't satisfying to him, and clearly not to the rest of the crowd. It didn't seem fair. "Does it seem fair to punish us for his actions, Captain?"

"I'm not punishing you guys. I would go back for you too. But I'm only going to stay and show you to the edge if you forgive Max. That's the trade. If you won't forgive him," Anna breathed slowly, "I can't forgive you. And I won't bring you to the jungle. Max could be in trouble, Boris too. When the

Sky-Lion's fixed, we'll go back for them before we leave."

Larraby stood and thought and sucked his tooth behind his yellow beard.

Someone in the crowd shouted out, "Go back for them!"

Larraby spun to see who it was. Others in the crowd were nodding and agreeing with whoever had said it.

"Yeah," said another, "the girl's right; we can't leave them!"

"What if it were you?" said another.

The crowd seemed to have quickly warmed to Anna's way of thinking. They were all in it together because they all wanted their freedom more than they wanted to hold a grudge. They all wanted to be on Anna's side because she was everything.

Larraby raised his hands to silence the crowd and hold Anna's barrage of innocent arguments at bay. He paced away from them all, thinking hard. He thought of how so many had lost their lives because of Maximilian's betrayal. How the Edges had almost been extinguished altogether because of him. How could he ever let it go? Anna made it sound so simple when it was anything but. The other Edges may not have remembered as clearly, especially the newer members, but Larraby could never forget what happened. Could never forget watching as the king's soldiers buried his closest friends alive.

How could such a betrayal be pardoned?

But if he could somehow manage to let it go, then Anna would offer freedom. Could it really be that easy—and that hard?

She would trade his forgiveness for a way out, for an escape from all the Edges struggled with and suffered from under the rule of King Adax. But what she asked for in return—it was so much. It was a weight that Larraby had carried for years.

Maybe the coyote was already dead. Or maybe not. But there was nothing in the world that Larraby wanted more than freedom.

He was so tired of hiding from the king and suffering at the hands of the king's soldiers. So tired of being in *the middle of the desert*. Nearly all his life he had been dedicated to the cause of the rebellion. He realized now, putting them up against one-another, that he wanted freedom with such wildness that any resentment against a traitorous soul, even any resentment at all, meant nothing. And then before he knew he was speaking, he had already begun.

"I'm in agreement with you all. If you can let the past go and allow Maximilian Howl back into our midst," Larraby shook his head sorrowfully, "then I can too."

Anna ran to him and gave him a hug. Her head came only to the middle of his chest. She looked up, "I'm happy you're seeing things my way!" Her carefree attitude returning, she realized how small she was next to him. "By the way, you're a lot taller than you look," she smiled.

Larraby looked down to her and squatted to her level to say something privately, "Captain, I don't know what you're doing. Or what you have planned, but I can feel you changing me. Changing all of us. It doesn't seem fair to me, to forgive all that he's done. Or it didn't seem fair to me," Larraby took a few breaths to choose his words, "but then I considered how I'd very much like the greatest pilot in the world to come to my rescue if I were in a steamin' dungeon."

"Bingo!" said Anna. "My point exactly." She spun around to the crowd and loudly proclaimed, "We're going back for them!"

The crowd cheered.

"Now," said Larraby, "how can we help?"

***

Back at the palace, things were not going as well for Maximilian Howl. His escape with Boris had failed and cost more than he could have imagined.

Boris the Brute was dead—yet another member of the Edges taken by the king's evil hands. Maximilian thought back to when their first hideout had been compromised. It was an underground bunker in a village not too far from Dung Dune City. The king had given Maximilian a choice—save the lives of his own family, his father and mother and brothers, or give up the location of the Edges.

Either choice would leave an irremovable stain on his conscience. But he couldn't willingly let his family be killed for the sake of the rebellion. So he gave the king the location of the Edges' hideout, hoping that, somehow, they would be able to withstand the assault. It was the hardest choice he had ever made, and it cost the rebellion dearly.

But ultimately, it didn't matter, for in the end the king broke his promise and took the lives of all of his family members regardless. Now, because of another of Maximilian's choices and because of his assurances that an escape would work, Boris too, was dead.

Maximilian's heart was heavy, and his sadness and remorse were overwhelming.

To make things even worse for the coyote scout, Sheena, the king's right-hand, was trying everything in her power to make his physical pain match that of his heart.

After Boris had been shot, Maximilian, wounded and defenseless, was forced to surrender. However, rather than being taken back to the dungeon, he was instead transported to a high tower of the palace—Sheena's tower.

It was a place he had been once before and he had hoped to never return. It was the highest point in all of Dung Dune City. Its balcony looked out over the busy streets below. As the sun rose and set around it, the fiendish shadow it cast was a reminder of the evil that King Adax and his forces draped upon the city. Now, Maximilian hung helplessly—suspended from the high ceiling and strapped naked against the underside of a metal table. He waited as Sheena sharpened a razor beneath him.

"Where is the airship?" Sheena asked as she shoved her wrinkled face right up against his snout.

Maximilian was silent. He stared back at her, ears flicking.

"Are you trying to help the rebellion?"

"They're called the Edges—"

Sheena slapped him hard in the side of the head and grabbed his snout, squeezing his jaw together. "Why are you helping them? What do they have that you give your feeble loyalty to them?"

If Sheena had already known about Anna, he would have gladly said that she, this girl captain, was the reason for his loyalty, the reason for his hope. But since her very existence was still a secret, he had to stay silent.

Sheena took the razor and scraped it from Maximilian's neck down his stomach to his hind legs. His gray fur fell to the ground like ash. He winced as she pressed the blade too hard, scratching him all the way down. A few drops of blood fell from his stomach onto the stone floor.

"It doesn't matter if you tell me or not," Sheena glared at him with a wicked, yellow smile. "The king will find them and that airship with or without you."

Maximilian was breathing hard. He could feel the cool, dusty air across his now exposed and cut skin. "You will never find it."

Sheena spotted the scabbed injury on his arm where Burp had stabbed him. She mercilessly stuck a knife into it. Maximilian yowled as she twisted the weapon. Blood rushed out of his arm onto the ground.

"We will find the airship," Sheena threatened, "we will find the Edges, and we will *kill* every last member." Sheena's eyes went wide with evil pleasure, but her grotesque enjoyment was cut short when she coughed and turned away from him. As the cough became a fit, she dropped the razor to the floor and hurriedly left the room, slamming the door.

Maximilian was glad for the reprieve, however long it might last. He tried to twist in his straps to get an arm free, but he couldn't. They were too tight, and he was too weak. Blood fell onto the floor from his stomach and his arm in a steady drip.

As Maximilian looked at the pooling blood beneath him he thought, for the first time, about how he might die. He hadn't had much time to think about it before, but now alone and helpless in Sheena's torture chamber, thinking was all he had.

He saw his reflection form in the blood as the puddle grew beneath him, and he had a revelation. All this time, he had been hoping to save Anna, hoping to protect her by his faithfulness to her—by his silence in the face of Sheena's tortures and whatever else the king might throw at him. As he looked up at himself in the reflective blood-mirror, he saw how truly helpless he was—strapped against a table, wounded, naked, weak, and hungry.

How could he help this innocent girl? He couldn't help her. The entire situation had grown beyond his power. He had little to any influence left to him, and no doubt, Sheena would kill him if he didn't give up the information she wanted. This was the end. He hadn't been able to help Anna at all. She was the purest person he had ever met, and the only one left in the world who would be kind to him.

He had nothing left. But his helplessness had brought him to a triumphant thought. *No*, he said to himself, *not just an innocent girl, but a captain!* Captain Anna Tomahawk, the greatest pilot there ever was, the meanest-dueling and quickest-shooting hero to ever live. He wasn't going to save her—she was the one who was going to save him! She was more than brave she was fearless. She had an airship and the Edges were with her and the pendant, Maximilian thought.

The pendant!

Did it really give her the power to do anything? Anything good, that was? Maximilian thought about what she had told him that night—that she would never lie to him. The thought was all the comfort he needed. He knew it was true. It didn't matter if he could keep his silence. He didn't have to be strong. Anna was strong. He didn't have to be brave. Anna was brave. He didn't have to defeat the king or help the Edges or rescue anyone. Captain Anna would do all those things.

All he had to do was believe in her.

Maximilian closed his eyes in exhaustion as blood seeped from his open wound. He had to hang on. If he could just last a little longer she would come for him. He knew she would come for him.

CHAPTER 14

Captain Anna Tomahawk may not have looked like a master engineer, may not have looked like she could have created anything from scrap parts and broken pieces of a once great airship. But she was deceptively skilled. Deceptive not because of anything that she had said or done, indeed, Captain Anna would be the first to say that she was the greatest—and she wouldn't have been wrong. But rather, her skill was deceptive because of the perception of the people around her.

They deceived themselves into believing that she was merely a girl—a smart, good, and brave girl, but still—just a girl. And in doing so, they couldn't see her for what she really was, what she had told them so many times as directly as she knew how. That she was the greatest hero, or heroine rather, to ever live.

Now, after a week of difficult labor, the crew of ragtag Edges had no doubts about Captain Anna's ability. She seemed capable to accomplish anything.

It was truly remarkable what she was able to do in just that short week. She replaced the Sky-Lion's previous two thruster pipes with six brand new components, more than doubling the airspeed of the ship. The cloth dorsal blades, which had been ripped in countless places, she replaced with treated canvas that could withstand even the mightiest of winds.

Most importantly, the steam engine itself, which Anna had built many years before, was now repaired—and then some. The engine needed exponentially more power in order to add the passenger capacity that Anna wanted, and with the help of the Edges, she welded a new steam tank that quadrupled the supply of the Sky-Lion's sweltering, steam-powered output. All the changes gave the Sky-Lion what Anna called "the extra juice" that it needed.

Further adjustments were made to the control panel, allowing for an additional five gears. Anna was confident that the changes would be flyable, though, they had still not tested it in the air. The first time they had powered up the steam engine the roar of the Sky-Lion was so incredible that listening to the finished product, she thought they might have been able to add even more room for passengers.

The workers and Anna had in effect already added an entire level to the Sky-Lion by rerouting some pipes below deck from the middle of the ship's cargo-hold. Then it was simply a matter of clearing out the many remaining boxes of artifacts, stacks of scrap metal, and piles of clothing that Anna had collected on her travels and apparently dumped into the lower portion of the Sky-Lion without concern. With all the extra space, the underbelly had been converted into seating for more than a dozen people. Above deck, they bolted down more chairs, and tied ropes around them for harnesses. Maximum capacity topped over thirty people when they'd finished.

It was a challenging week, and they had been fortunate that King Adax's troops had not been able to find the secret location. The Edges posted scouts in concentric rings around the construction site, just in case the king's troops came close. There had been a couple of patrols, but none had approached near enough to spot the airship. The Edges had completed the mission.

The Sky-Lion was back.

She was bigger and more beautiful than ever, truly a sight to behold once again. Anna's final touch had been to paint a giant, green leaf on either side of the tail end of the airship. The images became an inspiration to everyone. All of the Edges, involved or not, had been constantly swarming the construction sight since they had begun. Now they looked up to the vessel with awe, their eyes big with wonder as they drifted into daydreams triggered by the images of the green leaves.

All week long Anna had told stories at night of the jungle and freedom and more fresh water than they could imagine. Crowds would gather around her as she retold stories of her adventures. She never stopped talking. Even during meals she had an audience. Everyone young and old liked to listen to her exciting tales, and she loved the attention. The youngest members of the Edges had even started wearing their goggles on their foreheads to be like her, and they would sit at her feet as they marveled at the world she spoke of.

Now, Anna was standing before all of them. She walked the deck inspecting bolts and kicking various beams and pipes, testing out their sturdiness. She had her hands on her hips, and left her red jacket unbuttoned, so it flapped in the desert wind as she strode around. People on the ground below looked up to her, awaiting her approval, her blessing of their work.

Marching to the side of the Sky-Lion, she looked over the balcony towards the crowd. She gave a wide smile and lifted her pendant to her lips to kiss it. "Looks good to me!" she said to the crowd.

Everyone cheered.

"Captain," Larraby called from the front row, "come on down. We've got something for you."

Anna took a few steps to the rope ladder that was hanging off the side, and then deciding differently, jumped from the deck of the Sky-Lion and landed with a puff of dust in the sand. As she dusted off her boots, her newly repaired pants, and her re-stitched jacket, she walked up to Larraby. She stopped very close to him, almost too close. "What is it, Lar?"

"We have a gift for you."

Anna gave him a curious look.

"During the nights when we didn't have the light to work on the airship, I had some of our craftsman make a special addition. If you'd permit it."

Larraby stepped to the side with a wide gesture of his arm, and the crowd of people behind him parted. In the middle of the crowd was an elaborate drape, covering something twice as tall as the young captain.

Anna walked up to it as dignified as she could.

"Go ahead," Larraby said.

Anna squatted down low and grabbed the drape by its embroidered edge. Then, jumping high, she threw it into the air. Before her stood a metal sculpture—a hull for the front of the airship—the head of a lion.

"I love it!" Anna squealed, practically hugging it as she climbed on top to investigate every angle. It had red paint in its eyes, and its great metal teeth shined in the sunlight. Its mouth was wide in a roar, and its mane swept backward as if it was already flying through the air. "You did good, Lar! Everyone, this is great!"

Larraby was relieved that she liked it so much. He had been stressed about it because she had shot down every other suggestion that the Edges had made for the Sky-Lion. "It's nothing compared to what you'll be doing for us. What you've already done for us."

"Well, I never really expected you to be able to pay me back, I was just being nice and helping anyway."

Lieutenant Larraby laughed to himself; some others in the crowd chuckled as well. "We'll attach it to the bow tonight," Larraby said proudly.

"And tomorrow we save Max and Boris!" Anna said.

"Yes, tomorrow we strike." The crowd went respectfully quiet as their leader spoke.

"We have to do one more thing first," Anna said.

Lily stepped forward from the group, "What is it, dear? What do we have to do?"

"We need more water."

"We'll have teams working all night to fill up the tanks. We'll use all our reserves from the hideout." Larraby said.

"I'm afraid that's not good enough, Lar." Captain Anna leaned in to Lily, "Lil, we need *a lot* of water." She jerked a thumb towards Larraby like he was the only one who didn't get it, but Lily was equally confused. Her whiskers twitched.

When Anna saw the confusion in Lily's eyes too, she had to sigh and redo her ponytail. "There's not enough water to get us all the way to Dung Dune City and back," she explained.

"We'll give it everything we've got, Captain Anna. There's no second chance for this mission. If it fails, the Edges are done," Larraby said seriously.

The crowd got somber at his words. They knew he was right. If the mission failed, then King Adax would crush them. He would blot them out until no trace of a rebellion could be found at all. This one strike was the only opportunity they had.

Anna shook her head, "That's exactly what I mean, you said, 'if it fails.' You got to have some enthusiasm, Lar!"

"We will dry the well in the hideout, every steamin' drop. We could even send runners to get more water from the surrounding villages." Larraby couldn't figure out how to be any more enthusiastic for the heroic, little girl. What more could they possibly offer her?

"It still won't be enough."

"Then what will we do, dear?" asked Lily.

"That's not a problem, just fill her up as much as you can!" Anna said, twirling a finger into the air. "Leave the rest to me."

Lieutenant Larraby exhaled. "You heard the captain," he said to the crowd. "Every bucket we've got available I want running up and down the well until sun rise."

The crowd scattered, half towards the metal sculpture to fix it onto the bow and half towards the entrance of the hideout for water.

With the sun brightly reflecting off the new face of the Sky-Lion it looked complete, truly complete.

In the meantime, buckets and cups and canteens and every possible container that could be found anywhere were put to use hauling water up and out into the open desert air and into the Sky-Lion's tank. But the mammoth team working the well and water supply for the steam engine quickly ran into trouble. What Larraby thought would take all night, in fact, hardly took till midday. The Edges' camp ran out of water much sooner than anticipated. The flow of water from the ground into the deepest well was slow, and they had already used up a significant number of gallons to fuel the Duster for their trip to Dung Dune City the week before.

There was still plenty of daylight left when the team drained the last drop out of the well. The only water left was the emergency ration.

"That's it," Larraby said to Anna as she watched the last few buckets being poured into the top spout of the Sky-Lion. They tightened down the hatch behind the final drop and climbed down. "Is it enough?"

Anna grunted and pulled out her ruby pendant, "See this?" Anna asked him rhetorically.

"Yes?" Larraby answered anyway.

"Remember what I said?"

"Umm—" Larraby froze, trying to recall her exact words.

"As long as I have this, I can do anything." Anna went on.

"Anything?"

"Anything good, and saving Max and Boris, that's good."

"But, Captain, is it enough water? If we never make it to the city, we can't rescue anyone."

"Just leave that part to me, Lar."

"I wouldn't know what else to do," the lieutenant said, growing frustrated.

"Come on." Anna headed towards the rope ladder and started climbing up. She moved so quickly, that she made it almost to the top of the ladder before she noticed that Lieutenant Larraby hadn't moved. "Come on!" she called.

Larraby snorted and dust came out of his yellow beard and mustache. He stomped over to the ladder and began to climb, his mechanical leg clicking. When he reached the top, Anna was already wearing her goggles and was strapped into the captain's chair. "Hold on!" She yelled and pushed a gear at her side down to the floor.

The Sky-Lion burst to life, the wings on either side started flapping powerfully as the oiled metal chains slipped through the body of the ship with ease.

"Runs like a beauty!" She yelled back.

Larraby was in a panic. He was looking around in every direction. People on the ground had all cleared away from the sides of the airship and were watching, confused and alarmed. Was this supposed to be happening?

"Are you holding on?" Anna called again, but didn't give Larraby time to answer.

She kicked a gear forward and pulled another back with her other hand. A propeller on the back started spinning loudly and powerfully. The half-inflated balloon quickly filled with hot air. The Sky-Lion pushed off its braces as it started to fall forward. Anna grabbed two more levers with either hand, "I warned you!" she shouted over her shoulder and all the noise. With a yank on both gears, the wings flapped, the propeller angled down, and the Sky-Lion launched into the air.

CHapTeR 15

As the Sky-Lion climbed higher and higher, Lieutenant Larraby's dread escalated. His beard was blowing in the wind as he gripped a chair, knuckles turning white from his tight hold. It was all he could do to hang on.

"What are you doing!?" he shouted to Captain Anna.

"I told you already, getting water!" she called back over her shoulder. "Come on up here with me!"

Larraby looked around for someone to support him. There was no one. He and Anna were alone on the ship. He took the deepest breath he could to try to stabilize himself, but when he attempted to stand up, his air-legs hadn't quite adjusted. He stumbled and fell towards the balcony, closing his eyes as he lurched nearly over the Sky-Lion's side. Instinctively he grabbed onto the railing before he fell overboard. Relieved his hands found something to hold onto, he blew a breath out. But when he finally opened his eyes, he was still leaning over the side. He looked down to the ground far, *far* below and rolled his eyes back in a dizzied spell. He grabbed tighter onto the railing, trying to calm his fear.

The Sky-Lion's engine was running at a loud roar, but slowly it started to ease up. It didn't seem to exert as much power to maintain its speed and altitude as it did for liftoff, the balloon and sails took over the work. The loud noise and clicking of gears all around him quieted, though it didn't fall quite silent. Being on deck of the Sky-Lion sounded like being inside a giant clock.

Larraby stood with one hand squeezing the railing and the other wound in a rope tied to the main mast. He just had to wait until he could regain his equilibrium.

Anna was sitting on her feet, crossed-legged in the captain's chair and steering with one finger as if piloting the Sky-Lion was as simple as sleep.

"It helps if you sit you down," Anna called back to him.

"I can't...I can't...move," Larraby stuttered out.

"You'll get used to it in a minute, but you better hurry it up. You don't want to miss it."

"Don't want to miss what?" Larraby asked as he released the railing and clumsily stumbled towards the metal seat next to Anna's. He sort of toppled into it as the Sky-Lion bounced a bit.

Anna looked over amused at his worried and panicked expression. "Don't worry, Lar, I won't let anything happen to you. You're as safe as a fox in a hole."

Larraby wasn't so sure that she was right. After all, the Sky-Lion had been a wreck just a week ago. This was technically a maiden voyage, and although he had some confidence in Anna, his fear seemed to overrule that confidence. Having never been thousands of feet in the air before, it was a rather reasonable fear.

Larraby suddenly realized that they had no map or any landmarks to identify their location. In fact, Anna seemed to almost weave through the air. Turning the Sky-Lion this way and that for no visible reason, well, no reason beyond her sheer enjoyment of flying. The lieutenant was starting to get nauseated.

"How do you know you're going the right way?" Larraby asked.

"I just do," Anna said.

Lieutenant Larraby looked at her unsure as his skepticism continued to grow. He wanted to believe that she did know where they were going, but it wasn't easy to trust her. She seemed to always stop short of a full explanation. A few more words from each of her little thoughts would help a great deal, he mused.

"It's not far," Anna said.

"What isn't?"

"The Blue River."

"The Blue—"

Anna clicked in her cheek twice and smiled.

"You can't be serious. Any river would be hundreds of miles away. We'll never make it."

"It's not that far," Anna assured him.

"Captain, I've walked this desert many times. We are very far from the edge."

"But you've never flown it before, right?"

"What difference does it make?" Larraby asked, upset.

"All the difference. And, plus, you've never traveled it with me. *I* know where I'm going."

Larraby huffed and slumped back into the chair, "I'll believe it when I see it."

"I know," said Anna, "that's why I brought you with. Look."

Larraby hesitated, not sure if he should lean forward again to look. It was part nausea, part doubt, and part resentment. He inched forward on his seat and squinted into the distance.

At first, he couldn't comprehend what he was seeing, couldn't believe his eyes. He rubbed them with the backs of his hands in wonder. It couldn't be. It wasn't possible. He had walked in every direction for weeks and weeks and not seen any hope of an edge. Under his leadership the Edges had sent countless missions and wandered the desert for years. Searching, always searching. Always looking for the way out, for the freedom of whatever lay beyond the desert—never finding anything.

But, somehow, there it was.

Beyond all reason and plausibility, in the distance on the horizon was a sliver of blue stretching across the entire length of the desert. Like magic, appearing out of nowhere. His heart skipped a beat, the shore—the Blue River! His eyes went even wider as the realization sunk in, and his mouth dropped open beneath his yellow mustache.

"Told ya so," Anna said.

Larraby had already stood, forgetting his airsickness, and stepped past the flight controls to lean against the top of the metal lion's head. He was speechless. It was the edge.

He could've cried.

Captain Tomahawk was familiar with proving people wrong, and she knew that it was best not to rub it in when they had doubted her. Besides, there was another small problem on her mind, "Okay... now...let me think..." She bit her tongue. "Hmm..."

"I should've believed," Larraby sort of mumbled. Anna didn't respond. He turned to the girl to find her looking all around for a particular control, her hands in the air. "What is it?"

"Huh?"

"What's wrong?"

"I thought I put one of these things in here that could—ah, there it is!" Anna excitedly grabbed a lever behind the steering wheel, "Nothing's wrong, Lieutenant. We got to see if she still floats," Anna said.

"Floats?"

"Yep, we got to land on the water to scoop it up."

Larraby didn't like the sound of that at all. The airship must've weighed five times as much as it used to. Parts that had been wood were now metal. Parts that had been metal were now *heavier* metal. It seemed unlikely that it would float, but then, it all seemed unlikely, didn't it?

The discovery of the crashed airship, the salvage operation, kidnapping the greatest hero that Highsand had ever seen, the revelation that she was truly the pilot she claimed to be, her joining the Edges, the escape from the garrison at Dung Dune

City, and now this—the edge of the desert, the way out of the middle of all of their grief and pain, water as far as the eye could see—it was all unlikely. It was all impossible. But it had *all* happened. And it had happened because of Captain Anna Tomahawk.

"It'll float," Larraby said confidently.

"How do you know?"

"Because you're here. And your plans, however confusing they may be to an old soldier like me, they seem to work. So it'll float, I'm as sure of that, as I am of my yellow whiskers." Larraby smiled at the girl with an appreciation that, this time, he knew would not fade. "I'm sorry I doubted you, Captain. Forgive me."

"Already did. Let's test it out!" and with that Anna dropped her feet to the ground and pulled back hard on a lever to angle the Sky-Lion's descent. Larraby's stomach flipped as they dipped down, and he rushed back to his seat from the bow.

Captain Anna's descent towards the water was sharp, almost a free fall. It wasn't until the Sky-Lion got very near the surface that she pushed forward on her controls and the wings angled back to straighten out the airship.

Larraby's face was contorting into the strangest expressions of panic, but the Sky-Lion, perfectly maneuvered by its captain, skimmed across the surface of the bright blue water, spraying water droplets dozens of feet into the air. The cool droplets fell onto the deck in a mist.

As they sped across the glimmering surface, Larraby calmed. He realized with relief that they weren't going to drop straight through the surface and drown—he couldn't swim, of course.

"Check it out!" Anna shouted to him excitedly. She grabbed two spokes of the steering wheel and cranked it hard to the side, the Sky-Lion dipped into the water on Lieutenant Larraby's side. He clenched tightly onto his chair so he wouldn't tumble into the water. "You can reach it now!" Anna shouted.

Larraby whipped his head around to the girl to make sure he was understanding what she wanted.

"Go ahead, touch it. Touch it!" Anna said joyously.

Lieutenant Larraby, clenching the seat with his other hand, leaned out towards the water, reaching low over the side of the Sky-Lion. The spray of water between his fingers and the cool refreshing temperature of the river splashing in his palm were invigorating. He felt alive. The sun sparkled through the spray. "It's beautiful, Captain."

She just smiled and nodded, already knowing.

"Let's fill up, we've got no time to waste." She slowed the skim of the Sky-Lion by turning it across the surface. After a moment, it finally came to a near rest, only rocking back and forth as waves from its own wake struck the sides of the craft.

Captain Anna jumped up with energy and walked towards a control panel of manual gears. Larraby followed her across the deck. "Okay, Lar," Anna started, "it's kind of hard to explain how this works, but whatever happens, don't panic. It's gonna be really loud."

Lieutenant Larraby tightened his jaw and gave a quick nod to confirm he was prepared for whatever was going to happen.

Anna knelt down to the deck and began to slide open a long compartment. Underneath was a series of increasingly sized gears. A metal chain wrapped around the smallest and wove through another two gear wheels in opposite directions before heading up the length of the compartment and coiling through the rest of the spokes. There were two foot-pedals attached to the chains on either side of the compartment.

"That one's for you," Anna instructed, hopping over to the other side of the opening in the deck and putting her booted foot down on the pedal. Larraby copied her, tightening the valve on his knee just in case. "Once we start, there's no going back until it's full."

Understanding, Larraby copied Anna. They simultaneously stepped down on the pedals on their respective sides. The chain clinked into motion, turning the smallest of the gears.

"Keep pumping!" Anna said as more gears started interacting with the first. The metal on metal meshing of the gears was a symphony of engineering sound.

Underneath the Sky-Lion a gate towards the stern slowly started to slip open from the top down, sliding into the water and opening the tank to the air and the river. As the gate dipped past the surface of the river, water rushed into the open tank. Anna stopped pumping, and the lieutenant followed suit. She ran towards the back of the airship and looked over the railing.

Water was pouring in fast.

Larraby came up behind her and looked over her shoulder. "How long until it's full?" he asked.

"Just a little bit longer." The Sky-Lion began to sink lower into the river as it filled.

"Can you swim?" Anna asked as they watched the water come in and felt the Sky-Lion dip.

Larraby shot her a unnerved look. "Why?"

"Just in case," Anna winked.

"I can't swim."

"Well, then you better hope this works."

Larraby gulped.

In a few moments the tank was completely full. The noise from the water pushing into the tank had silenced and they stood motionless on the deck. Anna didn't say anything. She just looked around at everything. Looked at the boards beneath her feet, then up to the mast and to her captain's chair.

Larraby didn't know what to do, "What are you looking—" Anna stopped Larraby's question by putting a finger to his bearded mouth.

"Shh, wait for it..." Anna knew the gate would automatically shut when the tank reached maximum capacity. The Sky-Lion's tank was counterbalanced to lift the gate on its own.

They stood patiently, silently. Then the hitching sound came, the gate slammed shut. "Bingo!" Anna shouted.

Larraby sighed out his relief.

"Come on!" Anna said as she ran towards the front of the Sky-Lion. "Back to Highsand!"

CHAPTER 16

Back at King Adax's palace in Dung Dune City, Sheena stood before the evil beetle king's throne. King Adax looked at her with a stern face. It had been far too long without any developments on the location of the Edges' hideout or the crashed airship or the attack on the garrison. Too much had happened without any progress. Time had slipped away from him, and now he and his forces were, no doubt, trailing behind. With nearly two weeks gone by since the hedgehogs had shot down the airship, he was certain that something was transpiring amongst the rebels.

Sheena was making excuses for the lack of information. "He won't say anything, Your Highness. Maximilian is absolutely loyal to the rebellion."

King Adax squeezed all four fists of his beetle arms. "You're not being *persuasive* enough. Howl has to know something."

"It has been over a week," Sheena's wrinkled mouth was trembling in fear of the king. "He has yet to say anything to help us find the rebels or the airship. If I press him any harder, Your Highness...he'll die."

"Then kill him," King Adax said mercilessly. "We don't have the time to waste any longer. If he won't cooperate, we don't need him. I never needed him."

Sheena's face twisted into an evil smile. "Yes, he is a waste of time."

"He has nothing to gain by helping them." King Adax went on, "Where did this loyalty suddenly come from?"

Sheena was quiet. She still had no idea why Maximilian Howl, who had long been easy to convert, had such a strong resistance now.

"The rebellion must have more than just an airship, Sheena, to give Maximilian this kind of hope in their cause. If they had built it themselves he wouldn't be so loyal. There must have been someone on that ship, and Maximilian must have seen them," King Adax mused.

"Then it must be someone from the jungle." Sheena was frightened at the thought. "They've come to kill us after all these years."

It was possible, the king thought. But it didn't sound right. All of the soldiers from the garrison had reported seeing only known members of the rebellion—Larraby and Boris, the most recognizable of the outlaws. Surely, if the jungle cities had sent anyone, they would have made their presence known by now. But why would they? Why would the jungle send anyone after so many years? More pressing was the question of why, if they had, would anyone from the jungle want to help the rebellion. The Edges were weak. Most of the members were inexperienced dreamers or too old to fight. Even their leader was a cripple, his mechanical leg a result of their first insurrection. They couldn't stand up to his army.

"What do we do?" Sheena asked.

"The jungle must be helping the rebellion," King Adax said, finishing his own thought.

"But why, Your Highness?"

"That's what I don't understand. Why would they join forces with the weak? Why help *them*? What do they gain?"

Sheena had no answer. Selflessness was something neither one of them could understand.

The king was aggravated. He squeezed the armrests of his throne as he stared at Sheena. "We've wasted too much time. If they are from the jungle, they must've made promises to the rebellion about a way out of Highsand. It's the only thing the rebels care about. They wouldn't help for anything less. I'm certain the rebels have the airship in their possession."

"Burp and Belch said it was destroyed, Your Highness."

"Destroyed or not, the inventory taken from the garrison storehouse is peculiar. What if they've repaired the ship?"

"But how, they can't know how to build an airship?"

King Adax was growing more and more angry as their conversation continued. "Of course not, you idiot. It's the same thing we discussed the day the engineers shot it down. The crew. They know how to build an airship." He snorted like a bull preparing to charge. "They could've built a second or third by now. We have to find their hideout. I won't sit idly by as my kingdom is sieged by my own supplies. This is the end of their hiding among the dunes."

Sheena started to respond, but the king kept on, "Kill the coyote, we don't need him. Send Albert and the other commanders in here. We're going to tell them about the airship." He paused. "We're going to send out a new search party, and no one will be allowed back into the city until that airship is found."

Sheena turned to exit from the throne room and caught a final glimpse of the king's eyes. She had never seen him so deeply angered. Not slamming things and shouting, but boiling over on the inside. He terrified her.

As she walked, a more immediate concern filled her mind, killing Maximilian Howl. As she moved down the hall toward her tower where the coyote was being held, she passed Albert, the jackrabbit-sharpshooter and top-ranking general in King Adax's army. He was sitting on the floor against the wall, casually looking through the scope of his rifle. She flicked her head back towards the throne room, to send him in. "Wants to see you," she mumbled as she walked by.

Albert watched her pass, following her only with his eyes, before getting up and entering the throne room. Sheena heard the jackrabbit shut the door behind her.

She didn't like to be excluded from meetings with the king. None of his advisors trusted one another, Albert and Sheena least of all. An all out war against the rebellion was the last thing the wrinkled woman wanted. She was too old to be much help in a battle, and since utility was all that King Adax cared for in his advisors, she imagined herself quickly becoming expendable. She wished that Burp and Belch had never shot down the airship in the first place.

She huffed, trying not to let the thought distract her. Finally, after all her efforts to get Maximilian to talk and all the tortures she'd put him through, she would be able to deliver his final due.

His death.

She hated the coyote. Hated how he adapted and how they needed him, despite their long denial of that fact.

Her gleeful malevolence at the thought of killing him was escalating with each step as she climbed the stairs of her tower. She entered the chamber, high at the top, locking the door behind her and sealing out anyone who might interfere with her cruelty.

Maximilian was detached from the table now. He was slumped over in a corner of the room, cowering as far from the door as he could and looking either too weak or too injured to move.

"Get up, Howl." Sheena seemed to spit his name from her mouth.

Maximilian's only remaining fur was around his head. His body was totally shaved. He was covered in blood. His claws had been ripped from his hind legs. His ears had been clipped with shears. Even his teeth had been filed down. Sheena had done everything she could to degrade him.

He didn't move. He looked dead.

"Get up, Howl!" Sheena's voice cracked in her rage.

Maximilian blinked his eyes open and looked up to the old woman. He was speaking through labored breaths. "I won't tell you," he swallowed dryly, "anything."

"I don't need you anymore, worthless dog! You're about to die."

Maximilian winced and made a slow move to stand. Blood seeped out of his hind paws as he rose. He stabilized himself against the wall. "Why don't you need me?" he asked, shaking and thinking of Anna, wondering if Sheena and the king had at last discovered the girl hero.

"Because you're a waste of time. We will find the rebel's hideout without you, and we will crush them under the fist of King Adax's army." Maximilian couldn't help but think how much Sheena was starting to sound like the king himself.

Sheena snarled again and walked over to Maximilian, grabbing his snout. "You have nothing. You are nothing. And now you will die, alone and unsung for all your belief in the rebellion."

Maximilian met her stare and snapped open his mouth, attempting to bite Sheena's hands. It was the last of all his energy. She released him and slapped him with the back of her hand, sending him flailing. He collapsed hard against the wall.

He looked up at her, eyes steady. Unafraid.

She turned away, crossing the room.

"It's not the rebellion I believe in," Maximilian said to her back.

Sheena ignored his words as she grabbed a long knife from a table. She stepped towards him with smooth, long strides, savoring the prolonged moment of Maximilian's death.

The coyote, unable to move, stared toward the balcony that overlooked Dung Dune City. Tears welled in his eyes. "I believe in my Captain," he said. The sky was clear and blue.

It was beautiful.

He shut his eyes, wanting it to be the last thing he saw.

Sheena moved to stand in front of him. She raised the knife above her head to plunge it down into the coyote. "Your life meant nothing and your name will be forgotten, Maximilian Howl!"

"The name is Max."

And in a slowed moment as Max spoke his last words, a noise, a loud noise, the noise of an engine roared behind Sheena. The crack of a pistol rang through the tower chamber. The knife in Sheena's hands sparked as the bullet found its target and whirled the blade from her hands. Captain Anna Tomahawk leapt from the deck of the Sky-Lion down onto the balcony! She spun her pistol around in her hand and blew the gunpowder smoke away from the barrel. Her red jacket was unbuttoned and flapping in the gusts of wind from the Sky-Lion's wing.

"Alright, old lady," said Captain Anna, aiming the pistol right between Sheena's eyes, "I'm giving you one chance. Surrender."

CHAPTER 17

"Anna!" Max shouted, rejuvenated by her appearance. He tried to stand, but couldn't.

"Hey, Max." Captain Anna said, not taking her eyes off Sheena.

"You came for me."

"Of course, we're friends aren't we?"

Sheena was both terrified and enraged all at once. Behind this young girl, an airship hovered over the balcony. Which meant only one thing to the evil advisor, the king's worst fears were confirmed—the rebels had fixed the crashed airship. Sheena could see other members of the rebellion on board, although, she couldn't identify any of them. "Who are you?" she asked.

"I'm Captain Anna Tomahawk of the Sky-Lion, and I'm here to save Max and Boris."

"You're too late, Boris is dead," Sheena said.

Anna's eyes narrowed and she took a step closer to the wrinkled woman. "Did you kill him?"

"No," Sheena answered honestly, scared and not knowing what the girl was capable of, "he was shot while trying to escape."

Anna's face softened. Her eyes shimmered as tears started to form. She wiped her eyes with the back of her other hand, never taking the pistol off Sheena. "Lar, help Max," she called over her shoulder.

Someone threw a rope ladder over the side of the Sky-Lion and Lieutenant Larraby climbed down onto the balcony. With his leg clicking, he ran as fast as he could over to Max. He took off his long jacket to wrap the coyote and, picking him up, started back to the airship.

"You won't get away," Sheena threatened.

"Yeah we will. And so will anyone else who wants to come with me."

Someone banged hard on the door to the chamber. "Sheena, open this door!" It was King Adax. "The airship is at the tower!"

Behind the door, the king, leading a whole squadron of gunman, was ready to take down the airship once again. The Sky-Lion, being loud as it was and being the only thing in the clear blue sky, had of course, been spotted entering the city.

Sheena wished now that she hadn't locked the door.

"We're up, Captain," Larraby called down to her from the deck of the Sky-Lion after they boarded. The airship hovered over the balcony, swaying in the wind.

"Don't ever hurt anybody again," Anna said to Sheena. "I mean it. I won't give you another chance."

"Captain, let's go!" Larraby shouted.

"Not one more chance."

"You will pay for this, girl." Sheena said.

Anna stepped back slowly as she looked to the bolted door. Her adventurous and curious mind wanted to know what was going on. She had heard the stories about the king, how evil he was, how violent and how strong, but now was a chance to see for herself if all she had been told was true. As she was thinking it, King Adax slammed four arms hard into the door, smashing through. He had to hunch over to fit through the doorway.

"That guy is huge!" Anna exclaimed.

King Adax stretched out, towering towards the high ceiling. His beetle horns stuck through his crown and his cape was thrown back behind his shoulders, exposing his black, exoskeletal body. Two scimitars hung from a belt around his waste.

"Anna, we have to go!" Lieutenant Larraby was screaming at her.

From behind King Adax gunman rushed out like a wave, taking aim at the Sky-Lion and Anna. Realizing that she needed to move, and fast, Anna fired off a shot aimed at King Adax's crown. It connected like ringing a bell and sent the king, big as he was, stumbling backward.

Then dropping into a squat, Captain Anna fired another four shots at the feet of the gunman. They scrambled for cover. Anna spun on her heeled boots and sprinted for the side of the Sky-Lion. With a jump, she grabbed a hold of the rope ladder and, skipping rungs, pulled herself aboard.

"Take it down!" King Adax shouted. The gunman regrouped and responded with a flurry of shots.

Captain Anna rushed to the controls and pulled up hard as the bullets tore into the wooden sides of the Sky-Lion, sending splinters flying into air. She angled the powerful airship's underbelly towards the tower as they peeled away from the balcony. The bullets ricocheted back into the chamber as they bounced off the metal underside.

The Sky-Lion took great, sweeping turns under Anna's guidance as they swerved back and forth above the city, dodging the array of projectiles from the ground below. Crossbow-bolts and gunfire went off with abandon, barely missing the sails and the hot air balloon that kept the ship aloft. But the Sky-Lion was too fast, too well maneuvered, and too high to be struck.

King Adax shouted loudly, leaning over the balcony—cursing them as they escaped.

When the Sky-Lion crossed over the outer wall of the city, Anna propped her sword into the steering wheel, locking the Sky-Lion into a straight course. Once she saw its direction would hold, she ran back down the deck to Max. Getting close, she dropped her hip and slid on her leg across the deck, hugging him tightly.

"Not so tight, Captain." Max said, wincing as he lay on his back.

"Right," she kissed the coyote's cheek, not seeming to mind that it was caked with blood. "Good to have you back, Max."

"It's delightful to be by your side again," Max said through obvious pain.

Anna blew the hair out of her face. "Did you see all that! I cut it even closer than the last time I saved you. Pretty exciting stuff, huh, Max?"

Max could only smile, relieved. He was happy to see the young heroine alive, safe, innocent, joyous—unchanged. He coughed some blood.

Anna wiped the red liquid from his snout with her jacket sleeve. "You're gonna be okay, Max. You're with me now." She stroked his forehead with her thumb.

The rest of the rescue party, Lieutenant Larraby included, gathered in a shocked and slightly confounded circle around the two reunited friends. "Captain," Larraby said, "you were incredible!"

"Thanks, Lar," Anna looked up to him with a satisfied expression on her face.

"But, why didn't you take the shot at the king or Sheena?"

"I always give 'em another chance first," Anna nodded as she spoke, as if she did this type of thing every day.

Lieutenant Larraby shook his head, amazed at her capacity for mercy—even on the worst of enemies. He looked down to Max, nearly dead but rescued. It was hard not to have compassion for the coyote now, especially after all Anna had said and done and shown him. It felt freeing to see the creature now and to have no hatred or anger in his heart. The bearded lieutenant felt compelled to share that he had let the grudge go, but it came out awkwardly.

"Maximilian, I've forgiven you."

"Max, please, call me Max."

"Max, I've forgiven you." Larraby paused. "We all have." He looked around to the rest of the small crew aboard the Sky-Lion. "And you're safe with us. You're welcomed back to the Edges."

"Thank you," Max said, "with my most genuine heart."

"Don't thank us, thank her," Larraby said, nodding to Anna.

Max looked to her, but before he could say anything she winked at him and fell onto her back with a laugh. "What an adventure!"

"It's not over yet, there is another concern now, Captain." Larraby looked back towards the city. "Saving Max has put every member of the Edges in serious danger. We've exposed ourselves to the king. Captain Anna, he's seen you. You identified yourself to Sheena. The king will raid every steamin' building in the city tonight, inquiring for your whereabouts. By tomorrow, he'll be sending troops to every surrounding village. Hunting for members. He'll kill them when he finds them."

"It wasn't worth it to save me," Max said.

"Sure it was," Anna said matter-of-factly. "And don't worry, Lar. I won't let that happen. I'm going to save everyone. And I'm going to stop that beetle." Her eyes had a fire in them.

The whole crew aboard the Sky-Lion spread wide smiles. There was something about the way Captain Anna said things—so assured. Her voice made everything sound like it was already true.

"First," Anna went on, "we gotta get Max back to the hideout."

Max was barely maintaining consciousness.

"Yes. Agreed," said Larraby. He turned to the rest of the crew. "When we land, spread the word as quickly as possible, every member from every village is to come to the hideout. It's not safe anywhere else." He looked to Anna to make sure his instructions were satisfactory.

Captain Anna nodded. "That's a good plan, Lieutenant. But there won't be time."

"What do you mean?"

"I'm going back," Anna said, standing and moving away from where Max lay on the deck.

"Going back?" Larraby said to her as she sat down in her captain's chair.

"I have to," Anna said over her shoulder.

"What? Why?" Larraby asked.

"The whole city saw the Sky-Lion," Max broke in as some others helped him into a chair.

"Exactly," Anna said.

"I don't understand. You say that like it's a good thing."

"Because, they're..." Max didn't have the strength to finish his sentence.

"Because they're not all bad," Anna finished for her tired friend. "And now that they've seen the Sky-Lion—"

Larraby realized where the young captain was going. "They'll want to join the rebellion."

"Bingo," said Anna and she smiled.

CHapTeR 18

When the Sky-Lion arrived back at the Edges'
base, a crowd was already waiting. They cheered
triumphantly when Captain Anna landed the ship
with finesse atop the dune that overlooked the
hideout's valley. But the celebrating was premature.

"We need help! Get a medic," Larraby called
over the railing of the deck to the people below.
Three or four members of the crowd stepped
forward and started to climb aboard to help.

Lily, the gray-haired cat, was one of the first up.
She spotted Max immediately and scanned the rest
of the deck. "Where's Boris?"

Lieutenant Larraby shook his head, indicating
that Boris hadn't made it. Lily seemed surprised. She
opened her mouth as if to say something and then
stopped. Without knowing why she looked to

Captain Anna, watching her for a moment. Anna was rushing around the deck of the ship, checking various valves and gears to make sure nothing had been damaged in the escape. Lily wanted something from her, some acknowledgement that Boris had been lost. But Anna didn't even glance up at the mournful, gray cat. Finally, Lily looked back to Larraby, and he shrugged with his mouth.

There was nothing to say.

She moved to Max's side, "What happened to Boris?"

Max struggled to answer, "Sharpshooter. Albert—" it was all he could manage to say. It was all he needed to say. Lily knew of Albert, everyone in the rebellion knew of the jackrabbit sharpshooter, the most merciless of all of King Adax's generals.

Lily flicked her tail and jumped off the Sky-Lion into the sand. She started walking into the desert. Lieutenant Larraby watched her for a moment.

The bearded lieutenant didn't realize how much time had passed when Anna came towards him. "What are you looking at?"

"Lily," Larraby nodded towards the cat, now just a tiny black speck in the distance against the backdrop of the desert.

"Where's she going?"

"I don't know. Boris was her friend," Larraby said after a beat.

"Mine too," Anna said. "I've got some good news though. The Sky-Lion isn't too damaged from the escape. I checked the steam tank, it's shot through in four places, but I can fix it. The holes should be easy to plug up."

"Good," said Larraby, still thinking about Lily and Boris. "Excuse me, Captain."

Larraby climbed down one of the rope ladders that had been thrown from the side of the airship and headed toward the base. Max had already been carried off the ship and lowered in a basket to the hideout floor—the same way Anna had been when the Edges first captured her.

When Larraby disappeared under the shadow of the cave's entrance, the young captain heaved a sigh of relief. Everyone had retreated underground, leaving her alone with the Sky-Lion and her thoughts. The sun hadn't set, but it had already been a wearying day. They had done it. *She* had done it.

Captain Anna and the Edges had confronted King Adax face-to-face and managed to get away. At the same time they had rescued Max and shown all of Dung Dune City the Sky-Lion. She knew that by showing the airship, she had shown the city hope, and, perhaps more importantly, that King Adax was a liar. He was exposed now. The entire city would hear about the airship, if they hadn't seen it first hand. It would prove once and for all that King Adax was keeping them prisoners in their own land. It was a visible sign that not only did the technology exist, but that there was, indeed, an edge to the desert and a better, freer place beyond.

Captain Anna looked out to the dot on the horizon that was Lily. Everything they had done had been a success in every way apart from a single loss—Boris the Brute. He had risked his life for Anna and the Edges, and he had lost it. It was the greatest sacrifice.

Thinking about it brought tears to the young captain's eyes. As an adventurer, which Anna surely was, she thought Boris' sacrifice to be both noble and heroic, but heroism and nobility didn't make it any less painful. The loss would deeply impact many hearts amongst the Edges. He was one of their best and strongest. His death showed how serious a fight the rebels faced.

Further still, there would be grief. When word of Boris' death spread, Anna knew they would have to grieve. More than being a hero to the Edges, Boris was a friend to them. The captain thought for a moment about chasing after Lily to comfort her, but decided against it. Anna sighed with her thoughts, knowing that sometimes it was important to be alone.

She buttoned her red jacket all the way, retied her ponytail, and jumped off the side of the Sky-Lion. She landed on her hip and slid down the bank of the dune. When she reached the bottom she turned, blew a kiss to the airship, and broke into a sprint towards the entrance to the hideout. Her sword and pistol bounced at her waist as she ran.

All it took was a single step onto the floor of the hideout and she was greeted again with cheers. There were more members of the Edges than she remembered. Many of their faces were enthusiastic for the success of the day, saving Max. Others were somber as they thought of their friend Boris. Lieutenant Larraby was nowhere to be found. She walked through the crowd looking up and down at new faces searching for a familiar one.

From the youngest to the oldest, the Edges all looked tired.

At last, someone grabbed her arm and pulled her to the side. "Captain Anna, Lieutenant Larraby is waiting for you."

"Lead the way." Anna said, glad to be pointed in the right direction.

They walked through corridor after corridor on their way into a back room of the hideout. The escort stopped at the door and motioned for Anna to go through. Lieutenant Larraby and some others were huddled around a bed where Max was laying on his side. He was struggling to breathe.

They had managed to wrap all of his worst wounds in fresh bandages and were helping him sip water from a bowl near his head. He still looked weak, but when he saw Anna he smiled.

"How ya feeling, Max?" Anna asked.

"Better already," he said weakly.

"You get your rest, Howl," Larraby cut in. "There'll be plenty of time to talk later, it looks like you'll recover just fine. Though, you'll be steamin' ugly until that fur comes back in."

Max smiled at the joke.

Anna didn't get it. "Why, I think he's a very handsome coyote."

"The handsomest," Larraby said, humoring her.

"Ugly or handsome, I'm simply pleased to be alive. Where's the ship?"

Larraby helped Max sit up. "It's just outside, Howl. There's no steamin' use hiding it anymore, the king has seen it," Larraby said. "There's no going back now. That beetle will start his search as soon as possible. I expect it's already started. It's only a matter of time before they discover the base and attack."

"I'm mostly convinced he really is a bad guy," Anna piped in.

"Mostly?" Larraby asked bewildered.

"Well, I didn't get a chance to introduce myself. Until then, I'll withhold my judgment."

"Hopefully that never happens. We have to escape, Captain. *Now* while we have a chance. You have to lead us out of Highsand. That's the deal."

"Deal?" Max asked.

"I promised I would help get them out of Highsand if they helped me fix the Sky-Lion and save you."

"I see," Max said.

The room got quiet as some of the other members of the Edges looked at Anna suspiciously. Doubt was forming as to whether she would keep her promise. Sensing it, Larraby dismissed them. He hastily shut the shabbily made door behind them as they left. "You do intend to lead us out of Highsand?"

"Of course," Anna twisted her mouth to the side, "but," she stretched out the word, "like I said aboard the Sky-Lion, I'm going back. There are too many people who would be stuck here. It's not very fair to leave them."

"Captain, this could be our only steamin' chance to get out of Highsand."

"Don't worry. I'll show you how to get back to the Blue River."

"We're going to waste our opportunity, so that we can save the people of Dung Dune City? We've waited so long."

"Trust me, Lar," Anna said, taking Larraby's hands in her own. "I'll get you all out of here."

Larraby wanted to object. It was so hard to have faith in Anna's plans. Going back to the capital was crazy. How was he to agree to a plan that risked what he had worked his entire life to achieve? In his heart he knew she was right—it wasn't fair to leave anyone behind, but it was so hard to act on that truth. He tried to remember his trip with Captain Anna to the Blue River, how it had changed him to see it. He had to believe, as long of a shot as it was, that maybe if they saw Anna, the people of Dung Dune City would be changed too.

"All right," Larraby said, shaking his head. "What's the strategy?"

"I go back to Dung Dune City. Tonight. Alone. To talk to the king."

"No," Max said, desperately wanting her to never leave his side.

"Out of the question. We can't let you go alone," Larraby added in agreement to Max's objection. "You're too valuable."

"I have to go alone."

"Why?" her two friends asked in unison.

"Because I'm the best."

"That's not a reason," Larraby said.

"Sure it is. What? Are *you* gonna go?"

Larraby considered her words, "I don't want to let you go. It will cause panic."

"Listen, you can't *let me go*. I do what I want, I'm in charge, Lar," Anna spoke with authority. "Like you said there's no time to waste. The king will start hunting for other members of the Edges tonight. And you said it yourself, if he finds them, he'll hurt them. I can't let that happen. It would take too long to organize everyone, and besides, I don't need everyone. I'll be fine on my own. Just like I told you last time."

Larraby looked to Max.

Max raised his brow sympathetically.

"It's too dangerous," Larraby said. "How will you get out of the city if something goes wrong?"

Anna reached down the neck of her white tank top and pulled out the ruby pendant. "I'll walk out the front gate."

CHAPTER 19

King Adax stepped out the front entryway of the palace with an air of power and control. On either side of the beetle king waved two great red flags, blown by the wind tunnel created through the open palace gate. The scorpion insignias sewn into their fabric seemed to shake with the anger that emanated from the king. Around him in all directions stood guards and his highest-ranking generals and commanders.

He paused for effect before lifting his head and throwing back his shoulders. His eyes were cold and tight. The palace steps descended at his feet, and in the street below stood every living creature of the city.

He scanned the crowd with a scowl. In many situations like this one, a look is all it takes to intimidate a great many people. King Adax had mastered this look, and he was prepared to cast it. But then, in a strange moment of clarity for the short-tempered king, he eased. From the top of the steps in a sweeping motion he opened his four arms to the people of Dung Dune City as if to embrace them.

The crowd relaxed.

The king took a slow breath. He knew now was not the time for anger and threats—his usual tactics. He had to be careful, persuasive. The king was cruel and violent and evil, certainly, but he was also cunning. He knew that he was standing on the precipice of the potential downfall of his kingdom.

All because of a little girl.

The sight of an airship was an unprecedented event in Highsand. The technology had only been rumored, dreamed of even, whispered by the sane, and mumbled by the deluded. The implications of its actual existence were beyond anyone's scope to conceive. Seeing an airship, in the minds of many, was proof beyond all doubt that there was life beyond the world they knew, and they had seen it. *Everyone* had seen it. The airship was evidence that their hope wasn't an imaginative fantasy.

An airship meant that somewhere there was enough water and material to build and fly such a craft. It meant there was an edge to the desert. Meant that the people of Highsand need only set out for it, and they would surely find it. It meant the end of King Adax's power. The people didn't need him anymore. His ultimate control of the water of Highsand became worthless. If there was water elsewhere, if life could be better for the citizens of Highsand elsewhere, then why would they stay?

They wouldn't. The king knew that much.

And because he knew this, he was momentarily moved to withhold his anger. Sheena saw it in his eyes before anyone. She had spent the most time with the king, and now, standing beside him for this address to the city, she saw him become thoughtful. His brute force transformed into raw reasoning.

The scowl with which he looked down on Dung Dune City slowly faded, and as his countenance became totally neutral, he began. "My loyal subjects, what you have seen was not an illusion." The crowd was noisy. "What you have seen is my greatest invention." King Adax's mind reeled with the idea as it developed with each of his words. "As you know, from the garrison here in Dung Dune City, a supply house was raided by the rebels. They stole the parts and plans to build an airship that I myself designed. A masterwork of my engineering prowess, a vehicle designed for exploration."

Burp and Belch, standing a few rows of guards behind the king, looked at one-another, scratching their brows in confusion. The crowd murmured and began shifting, pressing in to hear. Sheena could've squealed in wicked delight, understanding the brilliance of the king's words.

"It took me years to develop the blueprint. I toiled for you, working in secret to create a wondrous machine, an airship. It was to be my greatest gift to Highsand," the treacherous beetle was shouting louder as he gained confidence in his plan. "I have given you water and protection from the desert for all these years. Now, at this crucial time when I intended to give you my greatest gift," he paused for effect, "a way out of Highsand—"

The crowd balked in disbelief, talking loudly amongst themselves.

"The rebels have stolen it!" the king yelled over the crowd's volume. "The rebels have stolen the freedom and prosperity that I deemed from the power of my throne to bestow upon you."

"You're a liar!" someone bravely shouted from the center of the crowd.

A guard moved to step into the street, but the king raised a hand to stop him and went on as if he didn't hear. The guard let it go.

"I hid it from you. I hid the airship's plan and construction from all of you because I didn't want to give you a *false* hope. I didn't want to break your fragile hearts with a promise I could not keep." When the king said this, the crowd began to go still.

Sometimes, when very few know the truth, a single person with only the power of a loud voice will be believed even when they lie. It is because of fear. It is this fear that kept the citizens of Dung Dune City silent. When the crowd grew completely quiet, the king knew it was because they weren't sure what to believe.

What do we know to dispute the king? What evidence do we have against him? They might ask. How would we know the affairs of such a powerful ruler? Why wouldn't he build an airship?

As King Adax mused about the questions they might be asking themselves, he began to answer them aloud. "Have I not given you everything you've needed? Have I not built a city from the dirt of a wasteland? Have I not given you walls and security and food for generations?" The king lurched down a few of the palace steps, getting closer to his audience. "Have I not let you do as you wish? Go where you like?" Finally, he addressed the one thought he knew was on everyone's mind, "*Who have I ever stopped from walking to an edge*, if there is one?"

Melancholy spread through the crowd as they recognized the beetle was correct. He had never stopped anyone.

But the city's people didn't realize in this moment that King Adax never stopped anyone because he couldn't. He was banished to Highsand, never to leave, and never again to know the way out.

The people of Highsand had long ago forgotten about the jungle. They had given up on leaving Highsand. They believed, as King Adax told them, that the desert was all there was.

But that had all changed when they saw the airship. The bright, green leaves that Captain Anna had painted on the sides had stuck in their minds. And the hope that had long since dried up grew alive again.

It was the rebels' fault, King Adax told himself. The rebels, the Edges, were the first to have that dead hope renewed. The first to go against his will, the first to dare walk out so far into the barren desert.

They sought the edge. Sought freedom. Sought the knowledge of a place beyond what they knew. Sought the place where he, King Adax, had come from so many years ago. Unwittingly, they sought the knowledge of what gave him all his power.

To conceal his true intentions, the king had gone so far as to encourage the citizens of Highsand to discover water, to settle new villages, to join his army and build defenses and towers that would protect the wells. He gave them controllable freedoms, illusions of having power over their own lives. And in turn, it pacified them to think they were being helped.

That was the lie that he had to convince them of as he made his speech—that everything he had done was for the citizens' own good, their own happiness.

He had built a world that they couldn't imagine without him. Believing him felt natural, because this manipulated world was all the people knew. For them to change their minds and instead of despair to have hope, meant contradicting all they thought they knew in order to believe in a myth.

A jungle?

From the middle of the desert, it was nonsense. The people found it so hard to believe in an edge— to have hope—that they couldn't see through the evil beetle's manipulation. Couldn't understand that through all of the efforts to look like he was giving, the king was in reality taking the most precious thing.

His words, like the scorpion he so wanted to be, were poison. "I want to protect you. All I've ever wanted is to protect you from these false ideas about leaving Highsand. Walking to the end of the world is an absurdity. That's why I warn you about the sand. It is a vast, cruel desert. More immense than you can imagine, and I do not want you to waste your lives wandering in it. I am not lying to you. I have done nothing but give to you."

This time no one objected to the king's words.

He breathed coolly, knowing they had taken his speech to heart. "Do not despair, my city!" The king turned and climbed to the top of the palace stairs. "Look around you, look at my army. This is the force that will wipe out the rebels once and for all. I will take back *my airship* to bring in a new age of prosperity and technology. With this airship, I will search out and find everything you've ever wanted, so that I can give it to you. We will destroy the rebels, and bring about a new dawn of unequaled power!"

Some of the king's troops began to cheer. Soon, the whole crowd echoed the excitement that King Adax held for vengeance upon the rebels. All because of his lies.

"We will search the desert," the king shouted over the applause, "and we will destroy the rebels!"

The crowd roared, and red banners with scorpions cracked in the wind high above.

But not too far from the palace steps, appeared a small brown boot across the threshold of the gate to Dung Dune City. It was quiet in the deserted streets; the only sounds were the flapping of the banners in the distance and the padding of the boots on the sand-dusted road. Step after step, marching down the main road of the city, the boots passed by statue after statue. Stone scorpions sat watching a sword bounce against a determined leg. It was a confident stride. Each step stretched the tightly worn pants. Over a patch on the upper left thigh, the hilt of a sword gleamed with an embedded diamond. The rough belt around the slim waist sagged under the weight of a holster and its pistol.

The figure, wearing a clean red coat, unbuttoned and flapping in the wind, approached the back of the crowd. Her white sleeveless shirt was a contrast against the sand-colored city. Around her neck, hung a ruby pendant, bouncing against her chest as she walked. Her face was steady, mouth sure and narrow. Her goggles were covering her eyes, and her hair was pulled back into a tight ponytail.

She stopped just a few feet from the back of the crowd and drew her gun.

CHAPTER 20

Captain Anna Tomahawk took careful aim, although to watch her shoot so easily it was hard to notice. With a loud crack of the pistol, she sent a bullet spiraling towards a gold ring that held one of King Adax's scorpion banners. The bullet ricocheted and sparked against the stone wall of the palace. The loosed banner drifted slowly to the ground, like a leaf falling. As it fluttered down near the crowd, people stepped aside to avoid being covered by it. The banner finally met the dirt street with a sound more felt than heard.

Like the ripples from dropping a stone in a lake, the people of the crowd parted away from the fallen banner until at last, the shooter was exposed.

Captain Anna lifted her goggles to her forehead and let them rest there. She still had the gun pointed through the separated crowd of people.

"It's her," Sheena hissed to the king, "the girl from the ship!"

"Shut up, I know."

Captain Anna knew how to make an entrance, but she had been so focused on doing just that, she hadn't planned quite what she'd say. "It's not your airship, it's mine. And I've got some questions to ask *you*, Mr. Beetle," she blurted out.

In all of the young captain's adventures, this was perhaps her most public confrontation. There were so many people in such a small area that she wanted to be careful not to start a fight. Even if she was sure that she would win.

"Why'd you shoot at my ship?"

"Do not call me *beetle*, I am King Adax, and I answer to no one!" King Adax stepped down the stairs towards the street. "Look at the thief, trying to claim the ship as her own," he called.

But the crowd already was. It was impossible for the people of Dung Dune City to take their eyes off Captain Anna. The great, rebel thief that they had imagined just moments ago was in fact, a little girl. It was an astounding revelation. But her gusto, her sheer confidence in the face of the *beetle king*, was a powerful testament to her own strength; this was the true leader of the rebellion.

Everyone in the city knew it. King Adax knew it too.

He sensed how ridiculous the young captain's appearance seemed to make his speech that had been so convincing just moments before. He was in a frenzy to explain her away. "Do not let the rebels fool you as they send a little girl to hide behind—"

"I'm no little girl," Anna interrupted him. "I'm Captain Anna Tomahawk of the Sky-Lion. And, king or not, *you will answer to me.*"

The crowd tensed.

King Adax paused and pulled back his head, tucking his chin. Everyone waited for him to respond with an outburst, but he laughed, unimpressed. "You are not brave. You are stupid, *Captain Tomahawk.*"

Captain Anna, though always quick to defend the honor of others, never got worked up about insults directed at her. She knew the truth—she was the best. So she ignored the king's remark about her intelligence and to prove she wasn't affected she twisted her boot into the dirt, not backing down an inch. "You killed one of my friends, and you," she turned her fiery gaze to Sheena, "you tried to kill Max."

Sheena pulled her yellow cloak tighter around her neck and stepped backward towards the guards. After her last encounter with Captain Anna, the evil, old woman was intimidated.

"I'm giving you both one chance, right now. Apologize, surrender, and promise to never hurt anyone again."

The crowd listened, astonished. Nearly a thousand people's thoughts could be summed up in a single question—*How was this happening?*

King Adax was incensed by the way this young pilot confidently gave him an ultimatum. His pride was under attack in front of the entire city.

"Apologize?" The king mocked, stepping down multiple stairs at once. "Surrender?" he stepped onto the fallen banner, his beetle foot landing on the center of the sewn, scorpion insignia. The crowd spread wider before him. "Or what?"

"Or face me."

"You don't come up to my belt!" The king seemed to bark the last word, violently shouting as his self-control reached its absolute limit. "I'll smear your guts upon the steps of my palace."

"That's it?" Captain Anna taunted. "Well, I've got more guts than you can handle."

Anna let the words hang in the air. It didn't matter that she was surrounded by troops or that King Adax was literally five times her size. She was as confident as ever. Her eyes shimmered over a smirk.

King Adax and Captain Anna stared at one another. Between them stretched a tension as taut as a harp string. The crowded people and creatures and the troops between every crenellation of the palace stood in silent, attentive wonder, watching as the huge beetle that ruled them stared coldly into the eyes of the young, fearless Captain Anna.

They waited for the sound of that plucked string.

The first chord that would begin a final song, a chorus of a change none of them could imagine. There are moments in time where so much happens in such a brief flash that the deep, deep significance of the moment cannot be understood until much later. This silent stretch of vision between king and captain was one of those moments.

It felt like it would never end. Time had slowed down, but then as casually as she could Captain Anna lowered her pistol, holstered it, and turned her back on the king. She could've done anything in that moment—well, anything good—but her decision to turn away was exactly what needed to be done to pluck the string.

The decision was fearless. It reverberated through the heart of everyone in the crowd.

The entire city watched Captain Anna as she placed her hands on her hips. "I'm leaving Highsand. Who wants to come with me?"

This was too far. She was too sure of her proclamation. Turning her back on the king was the ultimate, intolerable insult. She wasn't afraid of him. It was a slap to his pride—he didn't threaten her.

Instantly, King Adax's temper flared to life, like oil poured on a fire. He exploded with rage. A shout erupted from deep within him, a primal scream, the kind of outburst that you might expect from a lion or a bear. It was a roar of a shout. The two halves of the crowd spread apart even further as the king's voice seemed to push them back. Without a second breath, the king barked a command to his troops, "Seize her!"

A dozen guards rushed down the stairs of the palace, splitting into two single-file lines as they passed around the king. The crowd gasped and pushed and shook with excitement and fear.

Anna didn't move as they approached. They were only seconds away from closing in on her, each of them twice her size. One made a move to grab her, but she ducked and rolled away. She popped up to her feet as she completed her roll and spun to face the soldiers.

"So you guys know," Anna paused and drew her sword with a smile, twirling it skillfully back and forth across her body in a flourish of swordplay, "I'm really good at this."

The guards responded in kind, drawing their swords.

She twisted her boot in the dirt for sure footing.

"Get her!" one shouted and stabbed towards Captain Anna's head.

She leaned backward, bending at the waist as the sword came slicing through the air. Before the guard had time to change the direction of his attack, she swung upward with her own blade, connecting and twisting her wrist to break the sword free from the guard's hand. Her body moved fluidly as she spun a half circle, her hand popping up as she came near and landed a solid, jumping-punch underneath the guard's chin.

He stumbled back from the girl's punch and spit blood—and a few teeth—into his palm.

He looked up from the white pieces in his hand to another five soldiers waiting around to attack.

They were all as surprised as he was.

"Told ya," Anna said.

The five guards lunged at her at once. She rolled backward in a summersault faster than they could close around her and sprung to her feet with a hop. The two closest to her, one on either side, swung horizontally at her waist. She leapt into the air over the crossing swords and, doing the splits, kicked them both squarely in the jaw. They stumbled back as another rushed in from the center, swinging wildly. Anna parried the first few strikes as the metal on metal sound of the swords chimed across the crowd. Everyone around the skirmish watched in awe as the young girl danced around the guards.

Anna continued to counter the attacks, but one guard proved more skilled than the others. Anna was running out of room as she backpedaled towards the crowd. She reached across her body with her left hand and drew her pistol, aiming it at the guard's face—the same trick she had pulled on Lieutenant Larraby. But this time, the move was ignored. Without fear, the guard lashed out with his blade to strike the firearm from her hand. But Anna was too fast for him. Keeping her sword upright in front of her face, she spun towards the guard, closing the gap. The advantage of his long reach was taken from him, and Anna used the split second before he realized it to catch his wrist with the cross-guard of her sword. She punched the cross-guard up into his outstretched arm. It was the perfect angle for her, and the worst angle for him. Captain Tomahawk heard the bones in his wrist snap, and a moment later the guard's hand went limp. He dropped his sword, stepping away from the girl and coddling his broken wrist against his body.

It was just enough time for Anna to put her goggles back on.

Three more rushed in at the girl. They were refreshed after a moment of reprieve. All of the soldiers were bigger than she was and she knew that close proximity would give her a serious advantage, but not if she was surrounded. With the crowd getting dangerously close to the arcs of their sword swings, Anna knew she had to end this fast. Her eyes flicked to the sides as she looked for a way out of the crowded street. If she could fight the soldiers in the open or position them to attack her one at a time, she knew she could easily win.

With her pistol still in hand she swirled and parried blows from every direction, looking for an opening to aim. The multiple swordfights she was juggling were too closely matched for her to pause even a second. Her body was weaving back and forth between blades swinging so fast that they were nothing but blurs.

The dust coming up from the street was her only shield against the guards' powerful blows—fighting with goggles did have some advantages. As the sand continued to rise from the footsteps of Anna and the half-dozen guards putting her on the defense, she had an idea. In the cloud of sand, she saw an arm reach into the group of combatants, there was no sword, just a punch. She grabbed a hold of the closed fist and as it withdrew back towards its owner, she used its force to pull her into a slide. She slipped between the soldier's legs punching up into his groin as she moved to the outside ring of the fight.

Of course, the moment she was out of the center, the guards turned. The cloud of sand wasn't dense enough to hide her vanishing act. They squared up against her in a semi-circle as the groin-punched guard collapsed with a moan.

"Last chance, surrender!" Anna said.

"Don't let her get away, the king's watching!" a guard yelled, his face covered in sweat. The team of guards all started to move towards her again.

With dizzying speed Captain Anna twirled in a circle, simultaneously sheathing her sword and crossing her pistol back to her right hand. When she finished the turn, she came out firing. She shot to the left, then the right, then down the center and to the left again, hitting the guards one by one from the closest to the farthest away.

They all dropped or fell to a knee, as they clutched at their limbs in pain.

Anna, as fierce a fighter and a fight as this was, still wasn't ready to kill anyone. She thought about Max, and how when she had met him, he too had been working for King Adax.

One of these guys, could end up being a friend—if I give 'em a chance, she thought. Anna always wanted to give a second chance. So she had put bullets into their sword bearing arms or high into their thighs, completely shutting down their ability to attack.

The crowd stared in awe as Anna blew the gunpowder smoke away from the barrel of her pistol and spun it around her trigger finger. The hot desert wind carried the kicked up sand from the fight over the crowd, revealing how soundly the girl had defeated her foes.

King Adax, on the steps with the others, looked down to the young girl. His rage was pulsing from his eyes.

Albert, the sharpshooter, took a step past Sheena and lifted his rifle.

"Wait," Sheena stopped him.

Albert obeyed, slicking his jackrabbit ears down the back of his head and letting them spring back up. He didn't know why Sheena would want him to spare the girl, but he knew better than to ignore her command.

"Listen up," Anna shouted to the king and to the crowd, "I'm only going to say this *one more time*, I'm Captain Anna Tomahawk of the Sky-Lion. It's my airship and nobody else's. And you're a liar." She pointed at the king with her gun, "I'm not scared of you. I'm not scared of anything."

The king didn't respond.

The crowd was hanging on her every word.

Sheena continued to prevent Albert from taking the shot that would surely kill the girl; her wrinkled hand tightly clutched the shoulder of the jackrabbit's coat.

"I'm leaving," Anna said, then realized she needed to clarify, "leaving Highsand."

Some people in the crowd inched forward to hear.

"I'm going home, and anyone who wants to come with me to the *jungle* can come too."

The crowd stood quiet, desperately trying to understand what she was saying. It was too much to believe. It was impossible.

"Your Highness," Albert whispered, "I have the shot."

"No," said King Adax, barely turning his head to address the sharpshooter. "The girl is mine. She lies to you," the king called to the crowd. "Do not believe her stories of a jungle. She is from the dust of Highsand like we all are from the dust of Highsand."

"Actually, I really am from the jungle," Anna corrected him. Her persistent need to be right superseded her battle-infused mentality. "Why don't you believe me?"

"I believe you," said one of the wounded guards behind her.

Anna turned to the bloodied soldier. His peppered gray and black hair was matted to his forehead with sweat. "I believe you," he said again.

"That's great!" Anna said, smiling kindly at him. "Sorry I had to shoot you."

"I'm sorry for everything."

"It's okay, I'll bring you with me. Anybody else?" She turned back towards the crowd of people.

The crowd was still divided. King Adax stood with fists clenched at the other end of the hallway of people, and for a moment, no one moved. The crowd was like a rope in a tug-of-war between the beetle ruler and the young pilot. They were afraid of the king, and yet Anna was not. She wasn't intimidated, and her strength gave them strength.

Anna watched as the first person stepped out, a brave rhino. She winked at the creature in his brown vest, and he smiled and nodded in trust. Then slowly, person after person pushed their way out of the crowd to stand in the gap. They all looked to her. They looked to her sparkling, happy eyes, the eyes of their new heroine, as they courageously moved forward.

The dung beetle watched with growing fury. Soon there were hundreds filling the wide channel that separated King Adax from Captain Anna.

"To the edge!" one shouted from the middle.

"And the farthest shore!" Anna joyously responded.

"No! There is no edge! It is all desert!" This was it, sides were being chosen, and King Adax knew it. The people of Dung Dune City, his people, were turning to follow the girl.

"Follow me!" Anna said and turned to walk out of the city. The crowd scuttled behind her closely.

"Stop!" King Adax shouted. "Gunmen, aim!"

At the top of the palace steps from behind the giant beetle, two-dozen guards dropped to their knees and aimed at the crowd. Steadied rifles and bolted crossbows popped up from the crenellations atop the palace. The shooters holding them looked intent on killing. More soldiers appeared above the streets on the rooftops of the buildings.

"One more step, Captain Tomahawk, and you *all* die." King Adax smirked, knowing that he had won.

Anna and her new followers were surrounded.

They all stopped in their tracks.

King Adax stepped towards the halted group. "Did you think I would simply allow you to leave? To take command over *my* people?" King Adax reached down and drew two broad scimitars from either hip—they were each as long as Anna was tall.

Anna, ignoring the threat that another step would cause an execution, turned from the front of the group and pushed her way back through her new followers towards the king. She drew her sword with a flourish and fearlessly squared up against the beetle ruler.

"I thought you'd be smarter than to fight me. See, I'm the best, and I already gave you a chance to surrender. You didn't take it. You're still threatening to hurt all these people." Anna gestured not only behind her, but also to the crowd on all sides. "And I won't stand for it."

"You won't have to stand for it, but you will have to die for it. You should've listened to the King of Highsand. I said, *not one more step*." King Adax gave an evil smile. "FIRE!"

"No!" Anna shouted, realizing the danger.

But it was too late.

Gunshots rang out from every direction as bullets ripped into the group of new rebels. Captain Anna dropped to the ground to avoid being an easy target. Around her the rest of the crowd turned into a frenzied mob. There was chaos.

Screaming.

Running.

Pushing.

It was an all-out panic to get away from the gunfire. The group of new rebels scattered, scrambling for the alleyways.

Anna looked to where they had stood and saw spots of blood on the sandy road but no bodies. They might not be okay, but for now, they were at least alive. Now she had to protect them. She rolled onto her back, and kicked herself back up to her feet. The young captain wasn't up long before someone running from the crowd pushed by her, almost knocking her down again. Gunshots still cracked in the air above the streets.

"Stop!" she yelled at the king.

"Come die, girl!"

Captain Anna let out a scream as she charged towards King Adax. He was still standing above the crowd with a vile glare in his eyes. It takes a deep evil to be satisfied with doing wrong. And that's what King Adax was—satisfied. Satisfied with the panic and fear and death he had caused for so long. Even now, he was glowing with pride having given the command to shoot at his own citizens.

As Anna ran towards him, every step became drawn out. She wasn't even supposed to be in Highsand. She could have flown over the country without ever becoming involved in the misery of the creatures there, but it didn't happen that way. She hadn't let it happen that way. King Adax's evil had reached out of Highsand, even up into the air, into the life of the greatest adventurer there ever was. And that reach was too far. The proud beetle had brought upon himself a challenger greater than any found in Highsand.

Indeed, Captain Anna was not only a mighty, dangerous challenger—she was a heroic one. She could've left, could've flown away when the Sky-Lion was repaired and never looked back. She hadn't needed to put up a fight, rescue Max, promise everyone a way to the jungle, promise everyone a new life of freedom, but she had. She had done all those things, and she had given hope to the people who most needed it.

Now, she had to defend everything she had said. There had been enough talk. King Adax would never let the people of Highsand go free. He had to be defeated. As Captain Anna Tomahawk rushed in towards the ruthless beetle king, she felt the weight of each and every promise she'd made. She could taste the freedom of Highsand on the tip of her tongue.

With her eyes fixed, Anna defiantly raised her sword and leapt into the air towards King Adax. He didn't even bother to swing back at her with his enormous blades. He watched her steadily closing in on him, and as the curve of Anna's sword came down towards his neck, he reached up with both of his spare arms and caught the shimmering blade in two fists. His hard, exoskeletal palms absorbed the impact of the fierce attack with ease.

Outstretching his arms, he let Anna dangle from the hilt for a moment. Then as she realized King Adax's other two arms held his dangerously sharp scimitars, she released her grip and dropped to the ground in front of him. She clenched her fists at her sides.

The giant beetle looked down to the young captain, and without saying anything, he took her sword between two hands and bent it in half.

Anna watched in horror as her lifelong weapon was destroyed.

Chapter 21

King Adax threw Captain Anna's bent rapier at her feet. The point of the sword was curved so far around that it touched the pommel.

Anna was in disbelief. In all of her adventures, she'd never fought someone so strong. Her sword was unbreakable. She'd swung it against solid rock before and not so much as chipped it, yet the giant dung beetle bent it like it was a sapling tree.

King Adax wasn't about to give her any time to catch up with her thoughts. He punched forward with the cross-guard of his lower right hand. Anna saw it just in time and jumped backward to avoid the blow. At the same time, she made a move for her pistol and swiftly took aim at King Adax's chest. The inertia from his punch was still carrying him forward and she had the advantage of being small enough in stature that he had to bend down to reach her. When he hunched forward to swing at her with his other blade, he opened up his whole front. Captain Anna pointed the pistol at his heart and pulled the trigger.

The shot echoed throughout the empty street.

By now, the crowd had long since cleared from the shadow of the palace steps. They had rushed inside any open doors or under any awnings they could find to escape the gunfire.

King Adax staggered backward in the open courtyard.

Sheena looked down from the palace steps. Burp and Belch, the cowards they were, stared out from inside the palace gate. The soldiers in all their scorpion-decorated garbs looked down from the rooftops.

Captain Anna Tomahawk had shot the king.

Anna shook herself and took a few steps away from the giant dung beetle who stood hunched in front of her. She blew a stray hair away from her face and waited. Everything was still.

"Did she hit him?" Sheena asked Albert who still stood next to her.

"No blood," Albert observed.

"Kill her," Sheena ordered.

"My pleasure." Albert lifted his rifle to his shoulder and dropped to a knee. He was about to take the shot when King Adax suddenly straightened.

Anna smirked.

She knew it wasn't going to be that easy. There on King Adax's chest, right over his heart, was the bullet, lodged into his exoskeleton. There was an indentation and a hairline crack spreading from the spot like a spider's web, but the bullet hadn't pierced him. He flexed and the bullet popped free, falling to the ground.

She pulled the trigger another three times aiming for the same spot. But the only sound this time was the click of a pistol out of ammunition.

She was defenseless. Her sword—destroyed. Her pistol—empty and ineffective. All she had were her small fists and boots, and those would be no help against this enemy. She stood surrounded by gunman and face-to-face with the most powerful figure in all of Highsand.

She was out of options.

King Adax raised a sword and pointed it at the girl. "You're done causing me concern." He stepped towards Anna.

"Wait," she said, holding a finger up to her to ear. "Do you hear that?"

"Excuses won't save you now, girl."

"It's not an excuse," Anna said, pulling her jacket down and tight. "I *do* hear something."

"Enough!" King Adax stepped towards her and raised his sword for the final blow. Anna closed her eyes. There was no way she could dodge this attack. Still she thought she heard a sound. A rumble. An engine!

Anna knew immediately what it was. She opened her eyes excitedly, and just as she did, the Duster came barreling through a side street.

Lieutenant Larraby was at the controls. The top cabin was filled with members of the Edges and in the back were dozens more, seated as tightly as possible. They steered right at King Adax. Without slowing in the slightest, they crashed into the beetle and sent him flailing in the dirt as the Duster skidded to a stop in front of the palace steps.

Larraby jerked the wheel sideways so the tail end of the vehicle faced the palace. The Edges immediately jumped out of the back and started up the steps—swords and guns in hand.

"Take them down! Take them down! Kill them all!" Sheena screamed from the steps.

"Captain," Larraby called down, "catch!"

Anna snagged her leather pack out of the air as she ran towards the Duster. She dove headfirst underneath the front and crawled further in to where she would be protected from the gunfire. They wouldn't be able to shoot her with the metal tread of the Duster protecting her on either side.

Larraby jumped and landed in a puff of sand at the front where Anna had ducked under. The gage on his knee spun like a pinwheel as the impact from his landing overheated his mechanical leg. Gunfire snapped at the ground all around him.

Instinctively, he dove underneath and scooted in towards the girl. From his stomach he looked up to Anna.

She sat up with her legs crossed rummaging through her bag for more ammunition. "Nice dive," she said.

Larraby propped himself up on his elbows, pushing his goggles onto his forehead. "Just doing like you did."

Anna smiled. "I'm glad to see you, Lar. It was about to get serious out there."

Bullets were ricocheting off the inside of the metal tread. Larraby flinched as a stray bullet bounced behind his head. "It seems pretty steamin' serious already. I thought you'd be upset that we followed you."

"Nope, you came back for a friend." Anna gestured with her gun at the lieutenant, "You did the right thing. It's always right to do the right thing."

Larraby gave a slow nod, gently redirecting her pistol away with his hand. "Good. We have to move fast. That hit won't keep the king down for long."

"Right. I'll take care of him." Anna finished putting the last round in her pistol. "You help the others."

"Yes, Captain!"

"Ya ready?"

Larraby nodded.

"Here we go!" Anna and Larraby scrambled from underneath the Duster shooting wildly towards the rooftops. Larraby's mechanized leg clicked away as he took a hard right. Around the back, the Edges were fighting their way up the steps. Anna made a diagonal for an alleyway. She had had enough of fighting the king in the open with gunman watching her every move. It was time to fight on her terms.

King Adax was just rising from the impact. The Duster had hit him hard, but his shell had protected him. It seemed ramming him with a steam-powered vehicle had only served to make him angrier.

Anna whistled to get his attention. "Over here, ugly!"

King Adax gave a bark of a yell and took off on all six towards her, following as she sprinted deeper into the narrow city streets.

Lieutenant Larraby and the Edges, using the Duster as cover from the opposite side, had pushed hard up the palace steps. The other members that had come for the surprise-attack were fighting fiercely. Most of them were engaged in one-on-one duels.

Larraby scanned the area for the target he most desired to fight—Sheena. She was at the top of the steps. She had drawn a long, slender sword from somewhere beneath her yellow cloak and was fighting one of his men—a young tiger named David, whose parents had long ago been killed for the cause. Larraby broke into a sprint up the steps toward the old woman and his powerful, feline compatriot.

Burp and Belch jumped out in front of him before he could get to her.

"That's as far as you go," Belch commanded.

Both hedgehogs had their short quills raised and ready for battle. They carried pistols.

"Drop your weapons, Lieutenant," said Burp.

Larraby stood with his sword at his side, pistol in hand. He couldn't take both enemies out at once.

Burp and Belch started to laugh, knowing they had the notorious leader of the Edges at their mercy. But their laughter was cut short as a boomerang came whistling through the air, knocking both of their pistols from their hands and sending the weapons tumbling down the steps of the palace.

Larraby spun to see where it had come from.

Lily stood up the steps to their side. "Go," she said, "take Sheena."

Larraby pushed past the two hedgehogs. Weaponless, they let him pass uncontested.

Burp and Belch looked up towards Lily. She let out a hiss and, with an arch in her back, flicked her tail back and forth readying to pounce.

"Run, *rodents*."

Burp and Belch looked to one another, then back to Lily. She snapped her teeth. They both looked at one another again and screamed as they ran towards the palace. Lily pursued them through the gate.

Larraby was only a few steps away when David, the fierce tiger, leapt at Sheena's throat. She fell backward to avoid his attack and stabbed upward, piercing David clean through the stomach and out his other side. David roared in pain as Sheena placed a heartless boot against his chest and slid him off her sword and down the stairs.

Larraby paused and knelt by his fallen friend. "David!" He put his hand across the wound. "I'm sorry."

"Help Anna," was all that David could get out in his deep voice. A lung had been pierced, and he was breathing blood. It filled his mouth and was running over his fangs as he instinctively licked it back up.

Larraby looked from the fallen tiger to Sheena.

"You will never leave Highsand," she said to the yellow-bearded lieutenant.

"You will never leave these steps," he said through his teeth as he rose.

"Die!" Sheena screeched and raised her sword.

Larraby lunged for her, stabbing wildly and swinging his blade as fast as he could. All of the years of injustice, imprisonment, and struggle fueled his attacks. Lieutenant Larraby thought about all of the family and friends that he had lost at the hands of Sheena and the king—hundreds who had died because of a lie. A lifetime of pain was inflicted on an entire country because those like Sheena were filled with hate. They wanted power, wanted glory, wanted to hide the edge.

Sheena couldn't stop the brute force of Lieutenant Larraby. She looked around in a horror for someone to come to her aid. But there was no one. Most of the gunman had left their posts in an attempt to follow Anna and the king, and those nearby were engaged in fights of their own. Sheena had backpedaled as far as she could. There were no more stairs to ascend. Her back was against a pillar of the palace walls.

Larraby managed to twist her wrist roughly, freeing the sword from her hand. The blade clanged metal against stone behind her. Sheena's mouth quivered in fear as she realized her defeat. Her eyes went wide. "Have pity on the life of an old woman. Have mercy."

"Where was your pity? Your mercy?"

Sheena just shook.

"You had your chance for mercy with Captain Tomahawk. You didn't take it. Now I have my chance for justice, and I *will* take it." Larraby grabbed his sword with both hands and brought it high over one shoulder. As he swung it forward with all his strength, Sheena let out an ear-piercing scream.

She screamed until she lost her head.

When her lifeless body collapsed on the stairs, Larraby turned his attention towards the rest of the battle. His chest was already heaving from the fight. In an instant he saw Albert, the jackrabbit sharpshooter. The marksman had climbed up a ledge and was lying down, sniping into the skirmishes. Every shot he took hit another member of the rebellion. His aim was perfect.

Lily came out of the palace gate with blood around her teeth. She spotted Larraby and the headless body of Sheena.

"The engineers are dead," she said and spit blood on the ground.

Larraby nodded somberly. "There," he said, motioning towards the jackrabbit, "I'll go with you."

Lily flicked her tail and pounced over a fallen soldier on her way towards Albert's perch. As he jogged behind the cat, Larraby spun the wingnut on his knee to let the pressure escape in hot steam. They hugged the wall to keep out of Albert's sightline.

When they got beneath him, Lily looked up to her leader.

Larraby knew what she wanted. He grabbed her under the shoulders and tossed her up to the perch.

She landed, perfectly catlike, and immediately batted the gun away from the jackrabbit, slicing into his back foot with her other paw as she did. It was a deep scratch into the muscle of his hind leg. He wouldn't be able to jump away with the wound. She grabbed him by the shoulder and shoved his back against the wall.

Albert, being a jackrabbit, kicked her hard in the stomach with his other hind leg. Lily stumbled backward on the top of the small perch. Twisting with flawless balance, she forcefully thrust herself around. She found her footing and hissed, retaliating with a swipe of her claws across Albert's face.

"That's for Boris," said the gray cat.

Albert smiled wickedly and drew a knife from a side pocket. He slashed at the feline. Lily dodged it as it came across her lower stomach and countered with a claw slash the other way. This time she made contact with Albert's eye—his shooting eye. He reeled back in pain.

She took the opportunity as he grasped for his eye to pin his head against the wall. She pressed one of his giant ears against the stone with her claws extended. Her five sharp nails punctured the fur and skin of his ear.

Albert peeked out from his now only good eye. "You're not better than me, cat."

"Well, you're out of the competition," Lily said and bit into the jackrabbit's neck. She held her teeth tight until he stopped moving.

Lily leapt off the ledge and weighed the scene. Albert's death signaled a change in the battle. Without the rain of gunfire, the fighting had swayed in favor of the Edges. Reinforcements from the Edges' hideout were coming up the main road of the city, and many people in the crowd, inspired by what they saw, were helping in the fight against King Adax's soldiers.

Not too far away, between the narrow walls of an alley, Captain Tomahawk ran as fast as she could.

Her booted feet shot up and down like pistons in the Sky-Lion's engine. She was fidgeting with her pistol as she ran, reloading and then casting her useless leather bag to the side in order to ease some of the weight restricting her speed.

The streets were all empty, but there were some lights glowing in the front windows. She looked into every lit room as she passed, not knowing what she hoped to see.

The young captain took a sharp right at a fork in the street and scampered up a short, dividing wall. At the top she threw herself over, landing on her back in a pile of metal scraps. Sharp points pierced through her red jacket under each armpit, and a large spike of metal poked out just above her head.

She looked up at the metal spike. If she had landed just a little higher on the pile, she would've been impaled through the back of the head.

She heaved a sigh. "That was close." She ripped herself away from the jacket, leaving it tangled in the scraps. "I'll come back for you!" With heavy breaths she stood and looked around. The alley opened to her left and right.

She could hear the loud steps of King Adax's six legs running across the stone street and the sound of his shell banging into the walls of the alleys. She spun in a circle trying to figure out which direction the sound was coming from. She looked up the right side of the street and saw King Adax turn onto it. They made eye contact.

"You can't run forever!" he shouted and jumped high, hurling himself through the air towards the captain. Anna turned to run in the opposite direction as he landed where she had stood.

She turned down another alley. King Adax lurched towards her with an open hand, almost snatching hold of her boot as she turned the corner.

At every turn she gained distance on the king, but on every straight road he halved the gap. King Adax was fast, much faster than it seemed possible for such a hulking form to move. He forced himself through the constricted alleys behind Anna, his body scraping grooves into the stone and brick walls as he shoved by them.

Only the young pilot's never-ending willpower kept her out of his reach.

Anna took desperate breaths as she ran. The king was right—she couldn't run forever. Running wasn't going to defeat him. She had to turn the fight in her favor, had to get back to the palace and help the others.

With a huge gulp of air, she pushed her legs to their limit as she cut corner after corner. Anna dropped her shoulders to take every turn as tightly as she could. She knew that she had added a few turns between her and the king, but she had lost her sense of direction. The streets were complicated. They had no pattern whatsoever, and she was used to seeing things from above. She no longer knew if she was running away from or *towards* the monstrous beetle.

Anna burst out of a side-street and into a small courtyard with a six-way intersection. She made a snap decision and headed for the brightest of the roads, but then something caught her eye—a low hanging awning over one of the side roads.

She got an idea and changed directions, skipping off the wall to keep her momentum. She broke into a sprint towards the awning and with all her strength leapt into the air and grabbed a hold of the top, pulling herself onto the awning. Once up, she ran the length of the beam. She kept her arms out to the sides to keep her balance until she reached the nearest rooftop, where she climbed higher, thinking that, maybe up high, King Adax would lose track of her.

Feeling a little safer on the rooftop, she paused a moment to look around and regain her sense of direction. The sun was setting behind the walls of Dung Dune City. In the opposite direction she could see the top of Sheena's tower—the palace—she had to make her way back to the battle.

Anna looked down to the streets again. With the sun now dipping behind the wall of the city, the sandy streets of the alleys were becoming too dark to see. No hero, not even Captain Tomahawk, wants to run through unfamiliar streets in the dark. But she knew which way she had to go, and fortunately for her, the buildings were close together. Anna ran to the edge of the rooftop and jumped, landing in a roll on the next building.

Standing and dusting off her clothes, she looked back to see how far she had jumped. "Whew! Now, *that* was a good jump." She rolled her shoulders, smiling to herself, and ran towards the next building's roof.

She jumped, but the brink of the roof was too far to clear. She landed roughly, slamming her stomach across the corner of the building. It knocked the wind out of her.

Her vision was lost in a flash of white pain. She gasped twice, three times, trying to catch her breath. She was slipping down the side of the slanted roof. Her fingers clawed for anything to grab onto, but the metal was too smooth, polished by years of wind and sand.

The rooftop was high above the street—too high to survive a fall. Anna slowly blinked, trying to recover from the burst of pain. She pressed her palms hard against the surface of the roof, straining to hold on. They squeaked as she continued to slide towards a fall, but she had slowed her movement long enough to buy a few seconds.

Her wrists slipped past the edge, just as she came snapping back into full awareness. She curled her fingers and snagged the lip of the roof with her fingertips. With a grunt and a grimace, she ran her feet up the side of the wall.

"That was *not* a good jump," she said to herself. As carefully as she could, she steadied herself on the slanted roof and looked back over the edge. Even in the dim light she could see it was dizzyingly high. She squinted with determination. This wasn't the first time Captain Anna Tomahawk had just barely escaped falling to her death.

Ignoring danger like always, the girl turned and headed for her next leap. She continued from rooftop to rooftop as she moved towards the palace. She had lost King Adax, leaving him searching the streets.

Finally, she reached a building that bordered the palace courtyard. She ran to the center of the roof and looked back the way she came. The rooftops she had crossed were empty.

Anna put her hands on her knees to catch her breath as she scanned the layout. It was dark, and the shadows were deep. The sun had set quickly.

From the center of the flat, metal roof she looked out into the shadows. The roofs of Dung Dune City sparkled in the moon and starlight, and she couldn't help but notice how beautiful the city was. It was peaceful.

There had been no sign of King Adax since she had climbed up from the hunt on the streets.

The night had fallen quiet. There was no sound of gunshots from the palace, no cries of battle, no shouting from the violent beetle. But as she listened closer, she began to hear some commotion.

Was it over already? Had the Edges won? Had they been defeated?

Dreading what she might find, Anna turned towards the palace and walked to the roof's edge. There was an orange glow of firelight coming from below. When she looked down, she spotted Lieutenant Larraby right away—he was hard to miss with his wide-brimmed hat and his long beard.

He was collecting weapons, swords and spears and guns from the soldiers of King Adax's army, and throwing them into a pile in front of the palace steps. The entire city had turned on the army. Anyone and everyone not wearing a scorpion on their shoulder had finally united.

The Edges had won the battle!

"Larraby!" Anna called, excited to see him alive and victorious.

The lieutenant and many others in the courtyard looked up to rooftop where the girl stood.

"Anna, behind you!"

Anna spun, drawing her pistol. Nothing. She whipped her head back and forth to check the whole roof—empty.

"Here I am, *Captain Tomahawk!*" King Adax said.

Anna stumbled back against the edge of the roof. She had seen many incredible things in her travels and adventures, but this—this she never expected.

King Adax was flying.

From the courtyard the king could barely be seen. Only the glow of torches below with the stars and moonlight above showed the truth of King Adax's power. When the crowd realized that it was their ruler in the air, there was a collective gasp.

He could fly! All this time, their very own king possessed the power to help them. All this time, he had possessed an ability that could have been used to find a way out of the desert. But he hadn't. He had hidden it. He spread the lies that they would never leave the desert. Never find a way out. He had built the lie that there was no edge or end to their suffering.

If the soldiers still had their guns, they would've shot the king down themselves.

King Adax looked down from the dark sky to Anna on the corner of the roof. He stared with murderous ferocity. He wanted to make a threat at the girl, but there was nothing for him to say. His lie was exposed and his army was defeated. His city was occupied by the rebellion. His most powerful subjects and loyal followers were dead. Everything that he feared would result from the rebellion had come true. And it was the pilot's fault.

He had nothing left except revenge. Nothing left but to kill Anna, the one who had triggered all of it.

He dove out of the sky towards the girl.

He was so fast that he was a blur to everyone on the ground, but to Captain Anna Tomahawk—the greatest adventurer there ever was, the meanest-dueling, quickest-shooting pilot there ever was, the gunslinger who could shoot a match head off its stick from a mile away with her eyes closed—he was an open target.

She baited him to come to the side of the rooftop and when he got close enough, she sprang forward away from the king's dive. He swooped past her and began to pull up, to come around for another dive.

But that was exactly what Anna wanted.

With his exoskeleton open and his wings spread wide, the soft inside of the beetle's body was exposed. He had unwittingly turned his back on the dangerous captain by flying past her.

From one knee Captain Anna took aim, and with both hands wrapped around the pistol she fired every bullet she had.

She didn't miss once.

Dark, yellowish flesh exploded out of the king's back as the bullets connected with their target. The king fell from of the sky like a rock and landed with a loud crunch in the courtyard.

Anna didn't hesitate. She leaned over the edge of the roof and lowered herself to a windowsill, to an awning, to another windowsill, and to the ground. The entire city was watching as she walked over to the beetle king's body. A crowd formed around them, careful not to get too close.

"Get up, Adax," Anna said calmly—almost sad.

The king shook unsteadily and slowly forced himself to stand and face the young captain. Blood dripped from his back and down his legs.

Anna grabbed the ruby pendant hanging around her neck and squeezed it in her hand. Then with a serious face, she untied the pendant and held it out palm up to King Adax. "It doesn't have to be like this. If you take this pendant, you can do anything good, just like me."

King Adax looked in her eyes. Looked at the pendant. "I don't need you or your pitiful mercy."

"Captain, look out!" Larraby yelled, but it was too late.

The king lunged at the girl, throwing his arms out to the sides as he smashed her beneath his heavy chest. A puff of sandy dust came up from around his body, and his wings folded back under his shell.

Larraby stepped back in horror. The king had crushed her. The king had crushed her!

Captain Anna was dead.

The Edges and the crowd looked around in confused terror. How could this have happened? Why hadn't she moved? Why did she get so close? What would they do now? Anna was the only one who could fly the Sky-Lion. After all of this, it didn't matter. None of it mattered. They were still trapped in Highsand.

Suddenly, King Adax started to move. He leaned towards his right side and stopped, not quite pushing himself up enough to stand.

Larraby took another step away, terrified. "How could he have survived that fall? The gunshots? It's impossible."

"He's invincible!" cried someone from the crowd, horrified.

King Adax moved to stand a little more and paused again. Then came the voice, "Hey! Get this beetle off of me!"

Larraby's breath caught in his throat. He ran to the side of King Adax's body. Captain Anna was pinned underneath him, but she was still alive! He squatted down and tried to lift the carcass off, but with only one strong leg he couldn't do it.

He heaved with all his might as his mechanical leg strained to the point of near breaking. The wingnut on his knee spun wildly as his feet kept slipping on the dusty courtyard. His hands couldn't get a grip with all the blood.

"Quickly, help!" the bearded leader called.

People from the crowd hesitated.

"Quickly!" Larraby urged.

The crowd was afraid.

"She'll be crushed," Larraby said, filled with emotion. "You must help. Stop being such steamin' cowards!" he shouted, raging at them for their fear.

The crowd took a second look to make sure the king wasn't getting up. They watched as Larraby struggled further to lift the body. Listened as he screamed as he strained.

He couldn't do it. The bearded lieutenant dropped his head onto the side of the dung beetle's body as he tried not to sob. He punched the exoskeleton shell. Then he felt a touch on his back.

He turned to see Apple and Truck, his two faithful subordinates. They nodded to one another and stepped in alongside their leader.

"Thank you," Larraby said.

"On three," said Apple.

In unison, the three men pushed against the body of the fallen king, lifting it slightly off the ground.

"It's too heavy," said Apple.

"We have to get it off her." Larraby couldn't quit, not now. Not after all that had happened. Not when she had done so much for them. He couldn't give her up. So the three kept pushing, and as the crowd watched the men they were inspired with hope.

One by one a team moved in to help. Together with Larraby they finally rolled the body of the king over. Anna rolled with the beetle's corpse, seemingly stuck to his body as the team lifting him hurriedly stepped away.

When King Adax was flipped completely onto his back, it became obvious that Anna's arm was completely sunken into his chest.

Up to the shoulder.

With a disgusting sucking sound, Anna pulled her arm out of the king's body and stood up on his chest. She had used the king's weight against him. Used his rage against him. All she had to do was stiffen her arm and allow him to fall onto the spike of the ruby pendant. It pierced through the crack in his exoskeleton where the very first bullet had struck him.

She looked over to Larraby, Apple and Truck, then to Lily, and out to the crowd.

She was crying.

CHAPTER 22

The celebration in Highsand continued all the way into the next morning as the entire city sang cheers for the fearless Captain Anna Tomahawk. Their rescuer. Their hero.

She had issued a pardon for all of the beetle king's soldiers, urging the rebels to make peace. The Edges and everyone in the city were glad for the pardon. They were more than ready for peace.

The weapons were destroyed in a great bonfire, and the two sides danced and sang around the flame that represented an end to all the pain that had so long afflicted the desert.

Anna took King Adax's crown and buried it at the foot of the palace steps, saying that no one should ever uncover it. No king would ever be needed in Highsand again.

Messengers were sent to all of the surrounding villages to tell of the beetle's defeat.

Anna returned to the hideout alone so that she could tell Max the great news herself, that the bad guys were defeated, and that he was a free coyote once again, him and all of Highsand. They were free. The joy it gave Max to hear the news, brought a phenomenon of healing. He even managed to stand on his own to give Anna a great hug.

Together, they flew back to the palace, where Lieutenant Larraby and the Edges were cleaning up after the battle. There were many graves to dig and repairs to be done, scorpion statues to destroy and wells to open.

The Sky-Lion landed loudly in the center of the palace courtyard. Steam poured out from the valves on the sides. The crowd cheered and shouted for Captain Anna.

She leapt off the deck with a smile and walked up close to Larraby. "So, are you ready to go, Lar?"

Larraby looked around. "There's a lot to do here, Captain."

"Yep, they'll need a lot of help."

"You want me to stay," Larraby wasn't sure if he was asking or guessing.

Anna shrugged. "I've seen where you live. Now, I want to show you where I live. I can tell you're the adventuring type." Anna clicked her cheek.

Larraby smiled at the girl and knelt down to her level. "You are a wonderful girl, Anna."

"I know."

Larraby shook his head with a laugh. "I think I'd like to stay here for awhile. It's not so steamin' bad without a dung beetle in charge. I could help put things right—it's always right to do the right thing, isn't it?"

"Sure is, Lar." Anna untied the ruby pendant from around her neck. "Here, you'll need this. It lets you do anything."

"Well, anything good," Larraby and Anna said in unison. She jumped into his arms and gave him a hug.

"I'll be back to Dung Dune City really soon. But I gotta get home now, I'm bringing some friends to the jungle."

"Of course. Only, you can't come back to Dung Dune City, we're not calling it that anymore."

"What are you calling it?"

"City of Tomahawk."

"I like it."

"I thought you would."

"Where's Lily? I want to say goodbye before we leave."

"She wandered off again after the battle."

"Oh," Anna paused. "I didn't want anyone to die either."

"I know, Captain."

"Don't worry, I'll find her," Captain Anna saluted. "Goodbye, Larraby. Thanks for kidnapping me, it turned out to be quite the adventure."

Lieutenant Larraby's eyes filled with tears as he saluted. "Goodbye, Captain. I'll look forward to seeing you again."

"Alright, everybody, you know who you are! All aboard that's going aboard. We're off for the jungle!"

Max was already on the ship. He had taken the seat next to Anna up front. Another twenty climbed up onto the deck and strapped themselves in their seats.

"See you soon!" Anna called over the side as she pulled her goggles down over her eyes.

The Sky-Lion roared to life again. Its wings blew dust up high as it lifted into the air. Drops of condensed water from the engine sprinkled down as Anna spun the wheel and headed over the wall and out of the city.

"What do you think, Max? Ready to go to the edge?"

"And the farthest shore, Captain."

"I can't wait till we get to the jungle. You're gonna love it!"

"I'm certain that I will."

Anna and the Sky-Lion flew out towards the Blue River for nearly an hour when she spotted a figure in the sand below.

"We have to stop, hold on!" she called over her shoulder as she took a steep dive toward the sand below.

Those on board clung to anything they could find.

Anna skidded the Sky-Lion's metal underside against a dusty hill.

"I'll be right back, Max." Anna jumped off the deck of the airship down into the bank of sand. She started running towards the figure. Recognizing the gray fur and tail, she called out, "Lily!"

Lily didn't turn around. The gray cat had walked all through the night, miles and miles into the desert wilderness. With her enhanced feline hearing, Lily heard Captain Anna's first shout, but she didn't stop or slow down.

"Lily," Anna called again, "wait for me! Where are you going?" Anna asked, only a little way behind.

Lily turned sharply on the captain and hissed, "Leave me alone."

Anna stopped immediately, and the two looked at one another.

"It's your fault. If you hadn't come, Boris would still be alive," Lily said. "So many died."

"I know."

"Why does it have to be like this?"

"All rebellions are dangerous."

"I know that, but…Are we doing the right thing?" Lily asked, tears in her oval eyes.

"Yep."

"How do you know? You're just a little girl."

"No, I'm not. You know that I'm more than that. That even if it seems impossible, I can do it. You've seen me. I proved everything you wondered, even though I didn't have to. I did it because it was right. That's how I know this was what we had to do. That's how you should know, because of me." Anna was stern.

Lily didn't expect the young captain to speak so firmly to her, and now that Anna was, she didn't know how to respond.

"Everybody in Highsand is going to die eventually," Anna went on, "but not everybody will be free when they do."

"And Boris, was he free? Was David free? And the others?"

Anna gave a sad smile. "Yep."

"I don't understand." Lily said, still crying.

"Where I'm from this doesn't happen, Lily. It's so much better there. I have my own palace, and it's better than anything in Highsand. There is enough room for every friend I've made, and they'll all be there."

It was like the girl was speaking in a code that Lily couldn't understand. What was Anna saying? She looked at the captain waiting for more.

"Once a friend of mine, *always* a friend." Anna winked lightheartedly, and put her small hand on the cat's shoulder.

"Are you saying Boris is…not dead?" Lily asked skeptically.

"I'm saying, I won't be surprised if I see him again."

Now Lily was certain of only one thing—her confusion. Was Anna hinting at what she thought she was? Was it even possible? But then, there was something about the way Anna said all of it—so confidently and so kindly. It gave Lily hope that it was true.

"I don't understand," Lily said.

"I guess I'll just have to show you. We've got room for one more." Anna flicked her head back towards the Sky-Lion.

"You would bring me with you?"

"Of course," Anna said, "we're friends aren't we?"

"Yes," Lily said slowly, "I think we are."

Anna stepped forward and gave the gray cat a hug. "By the way, your fur is really soft."

Lily shook her head and wiped tears from her eyes with the backs of her paws. "I'm sorry I hissed at you, dear. I was just sad for all those who were lost."

"It's okay. I'm sad too."

Lily let out a sigh and looked up into Anna's sincere eyes. "Tell me, my young captain, what happens at the edge?"

Anna smiled. "That's the best part, it just goes on and on."

THE eDge

ACKNOWLEDGEMENTS:

This book would not have been possible without the constant encouragement of my friends and family. Mom & Aubre, thanks for reading the earliest draft—your enthusiasm and feedback made it so much better. All of my fellow writers & storytellers: Dan Aldrin, Phil Long, Brian Vance, Leslie Newton, Jonathan Smylie—you don't know how much you inspire me. My friends whose personalities I applied to characters and animals of various sorts: Elizabeth Walton you're as goofy and fun as the captain! Jason Schoenleber, Dad, Jane Hamilton, you're all the kind of characters worth writing about. Thank you to everyone who showed love for me and my book from the moment they reached the edge: Angela Beckefeld, Phil & Aubre (again!), Liz Fisher, and Sheila Hennessey for telling me the story is worth something. Kelly Hostinsky, you have been immeasurably encouraging and helpful to me; I could never repay you for all your enthusiasm and how much you loved Max. Ryan Clayton, thanks for reading it so many times, and letting me bounce ideas off of you at all hours of the night, you're an incredible friend. Alyssa Dunne, Jocelynn Fitch, and Neil Downey, I endlessly thank you for all your help at the finish line; you're all far too generous for your own good. Jill and Joel, thank you for being the greatest in-laws a guy could ask for. Brett Dlhy, Jim "Hooslefudge" Riley, Carl Fisher, Chad & Dani Keene, Jared Schrupp, Meredith Aldrin, the Wednesday night small group gang, the *Second City Saturday Superstars!*, and so many others—I love being friends with you, you make life better. You make me better.

Olin Kidd, thank you for the awesome cover, I love it; you captured all of the Captain's fun spirit. I hope she captures yours in return.

My biggest thank you is to my wife, Anna. Thank you for not flinching when I used your name as my heroine's. Thank you for reading and listening to page after page since the first day I was ready to share. Thank you for letting me talk through hundreds of ideas and for always listening. I love you.

What would I have done without you?

PLEASE GIVE THIS BOOK AWAY.

Made in the USA
Charleston, SC
28 August 2014